IN THE MIDST OF A DREAM

First published 2023

Published under licence by Brown Dog Books and
The Self-Publishing Partnership Ltd, 10b Greenway Farm, Bath Rd, Wick, nr. Bath BS30 5RL

www.selfpublishingpartnership.co.uk

ISBN printed book: 978-1-83952-608-4
ISBN e-book: 978-1-83952-609-1

Cover design by Kevin Rylands
Internal design by Andrew Easton

Printed and bound in the UK

This book is printed on FSC® certified paper

MIX
Paper | Supporting responsible forestry
FSC® C013604
FSC www.fsc.org

IN THE MIDST OF A DREAM

MARLEIGH HILLIER

BROWN DOG BOOKS

THE PREAMBLE

Coming towards the end of another day, you are feeling physically exhausted, yet your conscious mind is relentlessly active; vigorous thoughts and exciting ideas inhibit the peace of sleep. You choose to settle down with a book until you are completely relaxed and ready to slip into slumber. Comfortable and attentive you open the cover and begin to read. The sounds and sights around you dissolve into obscurity as you are absorbed by the words on the page into a different world, an alternate life.

Though you may not remember, you will most likely dream while you are asleep. Dreams are a constant and intimate part of our lives, though they remain a mysterious experience, providing a puzzle that is difficult to describe or resolve. Your imagination takes you to unseen places, to interact with unknown people, allowing you to live the impossible and sometimes the nightmare. You run, you scream, you fight and you fly; you breathe underwater and swim with the sharks, or you visit the moon and witness first hand its fantastic view of space, all this being possible within the vast realm of dreams. However, you are a victim of its whimsical nature; displacement and extremes are often the themes and you have no control over your script or your role. You are beyond the bounds of logic and law.

Relax. Breathe deeply and allow yourself to slide into your subconscious. Imagine you are about to go to sleep, because you are about to fall into the midst of a dream.

SUNSET

Softly, with the warmth of a summer's evening, the wind massages your face and you breathe deeply, holding, relishing the moment. Slowly opening your eyes again, you see the setting sun making the sky blaze red in the west while the east recedes into darkness. The clouds are becoming black, ominous objects lurking overhead. You must have seen the sunset countless times, sometimes watching intently with awe and delight, sometimes ignoring it, resenting its arrival as it is the constant reminder of time passing. It begins the countdown to bedtime and signifies another day over in your life. After years of familiarity it is difficult to watch them all. The setting sun, though often spectacular, is a constant that is often taken for granted. This particular sunset, however, is one that cannot be ignored. The sun is setting in a fashion that constitutes a cosmic event never witnessed previously, in a manner that has never happened in Earth's history. The sky seems to be rippling light shades of pink and green and the sun is becoming a tiny white dot above the surface of the planet. The clouds are receding, at an impossible rate, over your head to the eastern horizon. The harsh, cold wind that drives them buffets your face and stings your skin. You cannot watch; the water in your eyes may freeze if you keep them open. Protecting your head with your arms you crouch low and brace yourself against the ferocity of this sudden, dramatic change in the weather. Finally, it eases and you are able to raise your head and open your eyes. The sky begins to shift back to the accustomed blue, a brilliant blue, more intense than high noon at the equator. Then it is night; the stars twinkle brightly above you on the clearest, calmest night you have ever seen.

SLIP INTO SUBCONSCIOUSNESS

'This is Cassandra Banks. I understand you two have met.'

'Yes, we have,' replies Cassandra in an official tone, you just nod acknowledgement. You recognise her. The face is familiar though the name is not and you cannot remember where you know her from.

'Good. You will be working as partners on this mission.'

It is her hair. It is different. You remember her, vaguely, as having long, straight brown hair often held back in a band; now it is bleached blond, short and spiky. The green and brown camouflaged combat uniform suits her arrogant and aggressive demeanour. She stands, at ease, beside you, chin up and attentive. You notice she is clasping a black cap in her hands behind her back and the holster at her hip is empty. She must have handed her gun in at the clerk's desk before entering the office, as you did.

The silhouette of the Commander, sitting in his huge leather chair, is directly ahead of you. An imposing man of immense stature, what he lacks in speed he would make up for in pure weight and strength and he has a vast amount of military tactical experience to add to his wits. He stares out the window watching the troops training, using the glass to reflect his voice back into the bland, poorly furnished room. Explosions from the yard continually interrupt his monotonous rain of instructions, but you remain motionless during the pauses; picking out and memorising the important details of your assignment and ignoring the elaborate expletives aimed at the inept soldiers in between sentences. The Commander has been impressed with you and Cassandra lately, which is the reason you are both here receiving high praise and a long-winded list of orders. You leave the office upon being dismissed, and mull the mission over in your head. Dodging enemy radar, with the aid of ace pilots, sounds reasonable. Negotiating the hostile terrain and avoiding enemy patrols is feasible. Infiltrating the communications base and destroying the power generator by 0700 hrs, however, is a very tricky task, but you know you can do it.

Cassandra seems to be in a particularly bouncy mood, only revealed since leaving the Commander's office. She laughs, slaps you on the shoulder and says, 'Let's get it over with, we've got to get back in time to go on vacation. Jessica said she can make it and she'll meet us at the marina.' She signs for her gun and turns back to you. 'I'll meet you at the pad in forty,' she tells you before slipping through the stream of soldiers to the exit.

You take your gun off of the clerk's desk, thrust it back into your holster and then you sign the form that has been slipped under your nose. You slide the paper and pen back to the clerk, nod a salute and then replace your cap on your head before stepping out into the corridor. Other military office personnel are milling about hurriedly, walking stiff-legged and purposefully to whatever vitally important meetings they needed to be attending. You dodge between them heading for the main entrance. Cassandra has already gone through the double doors and is out of sight heading towards the barracks to collect her equipment. You are about to go the same way when the communicator band on your wrist starts to beep with urgency. You run out of the building into a corner of the courtyard where you are less likely to be overheard or interrupted.

Stacey never did know when to shut up, and now you are continuing this argument in the vacuum of space with only a double duvet to keep you warm. Yes, a space shuttle may come by any minute. Or an interstellar starfish with a good sense of humour might pass nearby and offer to drop you off at the Starbright Hotel. But, at this moment, the giddying effect of the stars and the severe lack of heat and oxygen preoccupies your thoughts to the point of fits of panic and vexation. How you came to be in this particularly awkward predicament is an enigma and how you are going to escape this situation is even more perplexing. A groceries delivery courier suddenly appears in front of you. He demands the sum of sixteen pounds and twenty-seven pence. This is for ten weeks' worth of back payments which he has worked bloody hard for; slaving through the damp rain and in the cold snow, up slippery ice and against the blowing wind and he is pissed off with you saying you don't owe him anything. He is extremely irate but he does not seem at all bothered by the absence of warmth and air. You keep trying to say something in response, but it is impossible to interrupt him. The courier just continues ranting and shaking his open, empty hand at you.

Stacey, in the meantime, is using the mobile phone to order a pizza. You hear the part of the order for extra cheese and pineapple, but as to what the other toppings are to be you are clueless. Instantly, a large yellow van with huge red lettering screeches to a halt beside you. A long, hairy arm extends out of the driver's window, passing a cardboard slab to Stacey. The hand then opens toward you and a fearsome, booming voice from within the vehicle demands the sum of sixteen pounds and twenty-seven pence plus a ten per cent tip. Delivery is free. Stacey whines bitterly about the service, the pizza being cold and the delivery taking too long and the rudeness of the delivery person, and then demands a lift back so a complaint can be made directly to the manager. You and Stacey squeeze in and the van zips off to the moon to a point where you can see an enormous, neon sign blinking on the surface, 'Neutron Pizza'.

Inside, the atmosphere is warm and the Neapolitan decor not too obtrusive. The music is of Latin style, audible over the chatter and not too loud, and all the staff seem to be in a pleasantly good mood. But the other customers stare at you from behind their menus or out of the corner of their eye. Outside, the vast emptiness of space is doing nothing overly exciting. Your reflection in the floor-to-ceiling, wall-to-wall window, however, shows that your duvet has gone. Before either of you has time to gasp with humiliation the waiter arrives bringing a clothes rack up to your table. He eloquently asks you to choose a garment to your liking and then for you to step into the changing rooms, behind the door to the right of the front air-lock.

The first thing you notice is the candle chandelier swinging wildly above you in an intangible wind. Observable through the unbroken far windows, above the mist shrouding the sea, stands the spiny castle on the cliff, glowing in the mysterious light of the moon. You close the heavy wooden doors to the ballroom and step back into the reception hall, your echoing footsteps emphasising the emptiness of the building. Invisible, yet opaque as an ebony statue, the creature continues to watch you. The beautiful tone of a woman's singing voice emanates from one of the doorways on the second storey. You approach the wide, winding staircase, carefully avoiding the loose tiles and piles of plaster, which have fallen from the unstable ceiling. The banisters writhe with life as you touch them, but they settle down to your gentle strokes and reassuring words. Each step creaks despite the thick, red, brass-tacked carpeting.

Bats have found a way in through one of the broken windows on the uppermost floors and they flap around the chandelier in a psychotic swarm engulfing the light from the candles and casting chaotic shadows upon the floor, walls and ceiling. The pitch of their chatter pierces through your skull and makes the hairs on the back of your neck stand on end. You continue climbing and the combination of sounds: the singing, the creaking and the squeaking, creates a chilling atmosphere in this silence.

The landing seems stable enough, though there are massive gaps where you can see through to the oaken beams and blackness beneath. There are four doors along the wall; two to the left, two to the right. Only one is motionless, the others open and close, erratically, of their own accord. You nimbly weave your way along the landing, gripping the banister tightly in your right hand, stepping delicately on the wooden beams where there is no floor, until you reach the inanimate door. It is ajar and the song comes clearly to your ears, louder, stronger and more enticing. The melody invites you to enter and the door swings open, politely, to let you in.

Bare, worn wooden steps lead up to an attic room where the warmth and flickering orange light escapes from a blazing fireplace, which helps to illuminate your way. You ascend thirteen steps and stand gazing into the large, open plan room. The fire is set back in the centre of the wall, to your right, surrounded by a massive, white marble mantelpiece. All along the same wall, paintings of lush landscapes and glorious sunsets are hung at varying heights, appearing like windows in comparison to the stark decor of the rest of the room. The walls are bare stone like that of the exterior of the building, the oak wood beams are exposed and the floorboards are left uncovered. The only furnishing is a grand piano standing in the light of the moon, that streams in from an open bay window at the furthest end of this narrow chamber. Beside the piano, sitting on the cushioned stool, is a young, slender woman adorned in a long, white, sleeveless dress. She looks out over the silvery landscape watching the fog rising up from the sea towards the ominous structure standing atop the cliff in the distance. Her shoulders sway with the rhythm of the song. You cannot comprehend the words that she sings, but you listen gladly to their soothing sound.

You go to approach her, but in your way you notice a strange mist gathering in the middle of the room, rising up between the floorboards and growing into a swirling column stretching up towards the cloudless, starry sky. The speed and volume of the song increases and the solitary voice now has harmonic accompaniment: a strange inhuman wail, deep and mocking, and there are others, of all ranges, excited and pained. The woman ceases singing, but the song goes on, rising in pace and fury. The piano begins to beat a discordant tune in misplaced tempo and the woman recoils away from it, wearing an expression of absolute horror.

The mist has a form. A huge form, with black, leathery wings, talons of an eagle and the torso of a giant, all resting on a plume of red, fluorescent smoke. The manifestation turns to you. The catlike eyes glare at you from the face of your neighbour. The smile is malignant and brief and you also notice your neighbour's teeth are much larger and sharper than when you saw them last. The Creature glides over to the woman in white. She is too terrified to scream, though she manages the motions. Staring at the images of her life flashing by, she can only allow the Creature to hold back her head and bite savagely into her throat. You watch, mutely, with no weapon to hand. Her head hits the floor with a gentle crack, the body hangs lifeless in the Creature's grasp, no longer convulsing with fear.

You will never defeat me. All who challenge me die.

The Creature's words echo in your mind. With wings unfolded, it ascends on an intangible wind and flies, with the body, to the spiny castle on the cliff.

'Killing them creatures is an obstreperous endeavour, always need a special way them, bloody things,' the Old Man tells you with convincing sincerity.

The old English style inn teems with enormous, sweaty, beer-bellied gorillas, who smell like they bathed in horse manure only a few hours ago. They are dressed in synthetic cow-skins and cowboy hats and appear to be out for a rowdy night on the town. Other patrons are cautiously attempting to squeeze between them to get to the bar. It is a busy night and the place is crammed to the point of discomfort. A troubadour is trying to prance around the crowded tables, strumming a lyre and dexterously avoiding punches. Your view is suddenly blocked and two frothy tankards of ale are slammed down on the table between you and the Old Man. A voluptuous, green eyed, red-haired, bearded barmaid scowls at you both and then asks gruffly, 'Do you want fries with that?'

'I don't want any, but please, you go with your fancy,' the Old Man says to you and minutes later, fries arrive with a side order of lettuce and live slugs; one is mortally wounded and losing a lot of fluid. 'You know what I think you should use?' he asks, after a while of pondering. 'A bloody great flamethrower. Incinerate the parasitic, blood-sucking monsters and spare no piss to put them out.'

You take a good look at the Old Man. He does not appear to be prestigious, wise or even very intelligent. His attire is as old as he is, worn and tatty, and his shirt seems to be adorned inside out. Facial hair covers not only most of his face, but is also sprouting from every visible orifice. The hairs spread from his ears to his eyebrows, then down to his beard, which bushes out below his chin. The Old Man's head looks like a big, white pom-pom with a stupid flat leather cap on top of it.

This, however, is a very animate and vocal pom-pom. A gruff, grumpy voice booms out from within and all the hairs jump about angrily. Occasionally the hairs part to reveal the sparkling grey and bloodshot red eyes that roll about maniacally behind them and a gaping mouth with rotting green, brown and yellow teeth. The teeth are an unattractive surprise when you are concentrating hard to try and see his lips moving.

The Old Man is a difficult fellow to follow in conversation. He seems to keep several trains of thought in mind all at the same time and switches between them without any comparative reasoning. He is talking about demonic monsters one moment and then about a sewing circle the next and then about the butcher and the greengrocer and then about the leaks in his roof at home. He also listens in the same way. You have spoken, briefly, about your skills and your friends and your future holiday plans and about some of your latest predicaments in everyday life all in tiny snippets in between his questions and opinions. You are about to ask him if he knows where to obtain a flamethrower when he suddenly digresses from the topic and starts talking about cats.

'My neighbour has got seven cats, you know. Disgusting creatures that know only how to hiss and stare and poo in your garden. My garden's a mess. I love gardening but I hate poo so, until my miserable neighbour comes to clean it up I can't do any gardening. I've a good mind to get a dog, a bloody big dog and I'll train it to eat cats. No, no, no, chasing is not enough. Not nearly enough. I might even train it to eats my neighbour's children too, that'll stop 'em climbing over my fence.' The Old Man lifts his mug to his fluffy head, drinks and then places it back on the table. You watch the foam from the beer dancing about on the ball of hair when he resumes speaking. 'I used to have a pet, you know. A pet dragon, of course. They're much easier to train and much more effective as protection. They do get big though, very big, and then loyalty becomes a bit of an issue. And people complain about cats clawing up furniture and curtains. Imagine, dragons like doing that too and if you miss a feeding time they burn your bloody house down. No, I think dogs are the answer this time. Two, maybe three bloody big dogs and I'll train them to poo in my neighbour's garden as well as eat their cats and children.'

You have given up trying to get a word in edgeways – the Old Man is enjoying the sound of his own voice. He obviously enjoys hearing himself talk much more than he likes seeing himself in the mirror.

'I like boating holidays myself. The wind in my hair and the gentle rhythm of the waves beneath me. And it is easy to get away from your neighbours. We should gather a few friends together to go sailing. There is a chap I know who will be very happy for us to go out on his boat with him. He's a nice chap but he gets a bit bossy, so watch out for that. Captain of the ship and all that high and mighty attitude. Doesn't help him win a poker game though. Oh, I can smell the salty air and hear the ocean waves and taste the rum and feel the coins jangling in my pockets, now.'

You can see that the Old Man has drifted into a reverie, still thinking his sporadic thoughts but only mentioning the occasional word rather than telling a tale or suggesting a plan. He and everyone else in the inn is suddenly distracted by a noisy commotion. Across the room, near the video game machine, a fight has broken out and has stopped just as abruptly. The first blows have caused a chair to somehow lodge itself firmly on the head of King Berthold IX, who is thoroughly distressed about the state of his crown. Several courtiers shuffle and grovel around the King attempting to disassociate him from the furniture, with great pain and effort, yet without much success. The initial brawlers are already in chains and are being marched away by large guards in blue uniforms and giant, silver helmets.

'Though a stake through the heart would probably be much more appropriate. Or using some kind of rare weed found only in the lost mountains of Arakar,' the Old Man resumes his vocalised pondering, now that the excitement is over and the customers and staff have returned to their previous activities. 'People are always itching for an argument,' he states, changing the subject again. 'Take that couple for example. One minute they love each other, the next they want to club each other with all kinds of furniture. Sex it is. That's the root of all arguments. Some people like it one way and others another and then some people don't like the way others do it and say so and others don't like the way they do it themselves and they stay very quiet about it. And then of course there are people who don't like other people even looking at their partner and others who like sharing many partners. If it weren't for the emotions and lack of effective medical treatments sex might be a pretty good thing.'

The atmosphere is disturbed again by the double doors of the inn bursting open, and a man dressed in a kilt and smothered in war paint, wielding a chainsaw, jumps into the throng. A space forms around him as everyone backs off from the point of the buzzing blade. He stares at everyone around him, waving the noisy, lethal contraption at anyone he perceives as stepping too close for comfort. He then announces that his name is Conner MacDonald and that he is the rightful heir to the Crystal Key of Rudarah, but he has lost it. Most of the patrons had not heard a single word of what Mr MacDonald had said, for the noise of the chainsaw had drowned him out. The smoke collecting in the room is also beginning to choke those standing nearest to the crazy person. Conner himself is coughing and moments later he decides to stop the saw. Between coughing fits he tries to re-announce what he has just said and then goes around each of the customers in turn asking if they have his key.

''ave yew goet et?'

WARNING. Altitude: five thousand feet.

The switches, dials, levers and buttons are all going berserk on the display in front of you. Even if you knew what each instrument meant, you wouldn't know what to do about it.

WARNING. Altitude: three thousand feet.

The cabin temperature is rising and the craft is beginning to shudder. Beads of sweat trickle from your forehead and drip from your chin. The view screen is a white blank and the steering column between your legs is behaving like a cobra attempting to bite into your groin.

WARNING. Altitude: two thousand feet.

If you've got anything to say, now is a good time.

WARNING. Altitude: one thousand feet. This is your last opportunity to initiate the ejection system.

Eject! So, which one of these flashing, bloody buttons is the eject?

Lost. You are deep in the middle of somewhere, but nowhere that you recognise. The tall, wide trees and the colourful vegetation, the steaming humidity and the vibrancy of life surrounds you. This tropical forest is a garden of glorious beauty that needs no tending, nor taming, just as nature had originally intended. In the shimmering, green canopy above, the birds chirp and hoot loudly at each other in an incomprehensible fashion and a group of monkeys are having a daredevil game of chase in the uppermost branches, crashing their way through the jungle, screaming fanatically as they swing. The sweet scent of countless, colourful flowers and the fragrance of the ethereal mist rising from the undergrowth after a fresh rain, enhances the air, creating a natural, euphoric feeling with every breath. Echoing about the tree trunks is the unintelligible chatter of insects, which is strangely soothing and pleasant, even comforting, despite the bad reputation they have built up. One of the vines near you wriggles and you are suddenly able to discern the pattern running down the length of it. The huge head of what is now obviously a giant snake lifts and moves toward you, its eyes staring, unblinking, into yours and, its mouth, as if you didn't know better, seems to be smiling at you. The python opens its jaw wide enough to swallow a car, yawning dramatically, before slumping back into its former catatonic state. You call out to Stacey and Cassandra and listen carefully for a reply.

Drums. It is definitely the rhythmic beating of drums that you can hear, coming from every direction, nearby and far away. The mass of trees shields whoever is making the noise and however many of them there are. The rustling in the bushes makes you feel nervous; the previously harmless lizards and mammals that moved them before could be a stalking group of tribal warriors intent on capturing trespassers.

There is a sharp pain in your neck and you reflexively cover the area with your hand. The pain increases as you brush against the object impaled in your skin. You remove it, quickly, and hold it up in front of you to see what it is. A tiny, red feathered dart with blood on its point.

One of the wonders of life is: how does such a primitive culture manage to build such an enormous iron pot? Stacey is not impressed either and is in a frenzy trying to operate the malfunctioning mobile phone with perplexing oral dexterity, whilst attempting to stay afloat and untie the knots. Cassandra's eyes are bulging with indignity and murderous intent. Only the vine rope prevents her from carrying out her desires and you are just coming round in time to witness whole cabbages, potatoes, carrots, turnips, beetroots, tomatoes, onions, peppers and coconuts being tossed over the rim of the pot to join the solution you are in. Outside you can hear the tribe chanting as they pile logs onto the fire that they have started and you can feel the warmth from it heating the water around your legs already. It is useless. The bindings are too tight, the situation too grave and the salt they are throwing in now stings your eyes like acid and you want out. A pole is lowered in and two well-built tribe people, with leafy coronets and flowery necklaces, begin to stir, making it very difficult for you to voice your objections. Near drowned and totally silent you stare up at the spinning tribe members as they withdraw the pole and disappear beyond the rim. You then slide into darkness as the lid is pushed over the top.

Temporarily blinded by the sudden daylight, you did not notice the bamboo and twine ladder being lowered into the pot. You are being beckoned by a young tribe person to climb up. Slowly, your eyes adjust and your befuddlement subsides and slowly, you ascend the ladder. Two large tribe people help you out when you reach the top and towels are handed to you. Two more tribe members, in grass skirts, throw petals over you as you dry yourself. A fourth tribe member smiles at you and says, 'Follow me. I will show you to your rooms.'

It is cold and damp, the fog and dew of an autumn dawn saturates into your clothing as you traipse your way through a recently harvested field. No one is with you and no one is nearby; you walk completely alone with no destination in mind, over miles and miles of gently undulating terrain. The severed remains of wheat and glistening strands of spiders' webs carpet your path and the earth below is soft and wet, from the heavy rain during the night, and you amble along with an added spring to each of your steps.

Upon surmounting the next hill, the slight breeze carries the whines of an injured animal to your ears. Your vision is obscured by the whiteness, but your instincts guide you to a hole in the ground at the bottom of the slope. Two metres in diameter and going straight down into black oblivion, the hole is a blemish in the landscape not of nature's making. The air is still and silent. Panting. There is a faint sound coming from the hole; the sound of a dog recovering its breath. You lie flat on the grass with your stomach to the ground, carefully edging your head over the hole. You can see no more clearly from this perspective than when you were standing up, it is deep and opaque. The enthusiastic barking from below suggests that you have been perceived as a rescuer. As you move yourself away, the barking sounds more pleading and you can hear the poor creature desperately scratching at the sides with the futile hope of ascending to freedom.

For five ... ten minutes maybe, the scratching and barking continues while you consider your options on how to help. It is quite a big dog: a Labrador, Alsatian or hound of some sort, this is what you would guess at by the noise it is making. Even if you had a long, strong rope, large pitons, a hammer and a torch, there is no guarantee that the dog would appreciate being bound securely, ready to be hauled out. It may resist or even turn nasty.

You sit watching the ants run between the green blades, full of incomprehensible purpose, and the two wolf spiders battling over a less than submissive cranefly. Shouting for assistance would only alert the birds to your distress. Going for help would be a good idea if you knew in which direction to head. The desperate barking progresses into howls of despair. Exhausted, the dog has ceased scratching at the smooth, black walls of its captivity.

Agitation compels you to stand and start pacing around the circumference of the perfectly circular pit. You walk around and around listening, reluctantly, to the pitiful cries, wishing for a solution to come to mind. Droplets of water hitting your face call your attention to the fact it is raining; a light shower accompanied by a chilling breeze. The fog will disperse soon. How long has this dog been trapped? The scenery is becoming more visible and you can see the hillsides spreading out, leaving you in a shallow valley that meanders out of sight each way you look. Patches of yellow and white flowers show through the weed-ridden, grassy slopes. The petals of the flowers are being stressed to the limit by the increasingly vehement wind and rain. The fog seems to have risen high, forming into dark, heavily burdened clouds. The aroma and bitter taste in the air confirm your fear of a serious storm. Intermittent barking. Quieter. Weaker.

There is no telling how deep that hole is. The conventional method of determination, by dropping a stone, is out of the question. If you try to climb down, could you climb back up? How deep is that hole? The hole that is, now, a well. A flash. The rain sizzles upon the ground around you, beating angrily against your head and back as you huddle up beside the shaft. You strain to hear the whining; you are shivering and the clatter of your teeth is drowning out, almost, every other sound. Decision. If you go for aid now, the dog may die alone, its last whimpers will be unheard. If you stay? The sky above rumbles and cracks; frozen water hisses as it hits the earth and the wind screams in motiveless fury. A soft, low wail, caused by the wind is all the sound that comes from the well. Ten … fifteen minutes, hours maybe, still no other sound.

The weather pacifies. It is cold and damp. All of the vegetation upon the slopes of the valley glistens with a ghostly aura in the light of an autumn dusk.

'Right, you and Banks go hold position in front of the gates and take out the guards when we make the distraction. Our objective is the science block; get in and then hold position there until the second unit arrives, understood? Good, you two are on your own, you know what you have to do. Good luck.' Sergeant Haynes whispers these orders to you before skulking off into the shadows of the buildings to where the rest of the team is waiting for him. Cassandra is ahead of you, moving stealthily down the street towards the main gates. Everything is still, everyone is asleep, as they should be at this hour. You weave your way between the parked cars and lampposts, keeping your head low and your eyes open. A cat leaping from under a van startles you, but you manage to refrain from shooting it. You relax as you watch the sleek form race away from you, across a garden lawn and then disappearing beneath a side gate. The house is suddenly illuminated from behind. A daylight security lamp blazes away, having been triggered by the cat's body heat. Cassandra rolls beneath a car, three ahead of the van you are standing beside; she is signalling for you to do the same. As you look up over the kerb, you notice that someone is peeking out from behind a curtain of the upstairs window of the brightly lit house. Two minutes later it is again dark and you crawl out from your uncomfortable hiding place and continue to follow Cassandra.

You feel certain that you will give yourself away with all the noise you are making; your footsteps echo between the buildings, your rifle and backpack slap against your body and your breathing sounds like a hurricane rushing to and from your lungs. Cassandra is running graceful and silent, with a perceivable skip in her stride. Two sharp, white beams of light cut into the yellow darkness of the street. A grocery delivery van is approaching from an adjacent road; the headlamps sending the beams over the stationary vehicles like searchlights. You crouch, tight up alongside the front wheel of a small sports car; Cassandra sits back and relaxes in the shelter beside the bus stop. The delivery van stops. It is facing your way. You hear the clinking of bottles as the courier prepares his delivery. You cannot sustain this position much longer, the smell from the drain you are leaning over is unpleasant and cramp is developing in your right leg. Finally, the courier walks up a garden path on the opposite side of the street. You limp, hastily, over to the bus-stop shelter and push Cassandra's legs off the bench. She eases the backpack over her shoulders again and stands ready to run the next time that the courier has his back turned. Moments later she is gone. Twenty metres ahead, on the left, is the road you need to enter. Looking back over your shoulder, you can see the courier has returned to his van. He busily sets about organising another round while you watch, waiting to catch the briefest moment to move without bringing attention to yourself. He begins to walk in your direction to make the deliveries on this side of the street. He passes your location and opens the squeaky little brown gate to the house with the immaculate lawn, directly in front of you. He proceeds towards the doorstep, carefully ignoring the paving stones provided for stepping on, and places the box, noisily, on the tiled floor of the porch, before heading back via another route through the flower beds. By the time he reaches the gate he will notice you. You will have to do something. He is just about to open the gate when he is startled by you lurking in the shadows of the bus-stop shelter and then again, a split second later, by the arms that have extended out from behind a bush to close around his neck. Cassandra knocks him unconscious and then drags him over the paving stones leading to the pond beside the willow tree and slides him into the water. She does not bother to shut the gate as she exits the front garden of number thirty-two; she runs to the next road, on the left, expecting you to follow.

Rounding the corner the gates become visible to you. The silhouettes of two guards pace back and forth behind the railings. In a hut, to the right of the entrance, the lights are on and you can only presume that there are more guards inside. You sneak a little nearer and find a suitable vantage point, in the garden of a quaint, well-kept cottage, out of sight behind some neatly trimmed bushes. Cassandra is also out of sight, but you know she is in a similar position on the other side of the street. The infra-red gunsight enhances the image of your target; you can pinpoint the white patch on his chest and stop his heart, or aim at the blue-green area between the red dots and pierce his brain. Cassandra does not have a problem with killing the enemy. She justifies it by stating the view that, 'They are fighting for a cause and they are prepared to die for that cause. They have lived life with purpose, more than most do regardless of their life being short or long.'

A Jeep pulls up and after a brief conversation with the occupants the guards open the gates and wave them through. The Jeep jerks away, swerves around the hut and speeds off across the court-lined playground, heading for the rear of the main building. The guards close and lock the gates again, and then resume their original posts, pacing back and forth, waiting for some action.

The ceiling of this corridor seems to be much lower than you remember it. The steps are also much smaller and you can, now, take them several at a time. So far, there has been an insignificant amount of opposition, but they would not have expected this form of infiltration and they will be in an incredibly bad mood when they discover you here.

Cassandra tries to open the door to the next classroom. It is locked. Peering through the glass you can see it is vacant;

only desks, chairs, books and a few cupboards occupy the space. The diffused, orange light from the street lamps passing through the classroom windows, on the opposite wall, causes the little plastic seats to radiate, vividly, like camp-fires set in a ritualised, grid formation. The big desk, nearest the door, is the only one with anything on it; pens, paper, folders and exercise books are perfectly arranged to one side, the other is bare, except for a ripe, green apple, being used as a paperweight for an unfolded note. On the far wall, at the back of the classroom, large sheets of white paper, decorated with wild blotches of colour and generous splatterings of paint, are crowded into a limited area forming a psychedelic wallpaper, almost nauseating to look at. Individually they would be called paintings out of kindness and consideration. The next door is not locked. Though it is on the other side of the corridor, the room has the same layout as the previous one. Cassandra checks the cupboards and drawers, but finding nothing of any interest you move on, further into the building.

Raising your rifle from your side to your shoulder in one fluid motion, you crouch down beside Cassandra and wait to see who comes around the corner. They are not alerted to your presence, yet. Whoever it is has slammed the main doors open, announcing their arrival and is making no effort to be stealthy. And it sounds as though there is only one of them. The moment they step into gunsight they will flare up like a 'Roman candle' firework.

The sound is a cross between slurping and gurgling, with a hint of spine chilling. There are no footsteps; instead, the noise is a shuffle or a drag, more like both at the same time. Whatever is causing these sounds is coming nearer. It is too late to escape detection. A dull, green blob appears in your gunsight, slowly, sliding into view, nearly engulfing the entire circle of darkness that you have been staring at. It is big, very big, too big to be rightly moving about freely within the hallways of this building. If it is aware that you are here, it does not care that you are pointing at it. The sharp zap of Cassandra's laser rifle discharge pierces into the green patch, switching from a blinding white line to a soft, blue tracer as the photo-chromatic element of the gunsight reacts to the intensity of the light. The blob appears to be undamaged and it will now be certain that it is in unfriendly, even hostile company. The rapid fire from Cassandra's rifle allows you to faintly see your adversary without the gunsight. It is not human. Nor is it of this world. The closest thing it could be related to on Earth is a giant snail or slug with a tortoise-like shell. A giant sluggy, snailly, tortoisey type thing: possessing two arm-like protrusions with long, tentacle fingers, and a huge bulbous head with three probing tendrils wriggling from the face of it. The slimy, soft, green and black upper body of the alien quickly retracts into the impregnable, spiny, magenta, blue and yellow striped exo-skeletal armour.

'Cover me,' is all Cassandra says before crawling her way towards the inanimate dome. You are careful to bounce your shots towards the ceiling, so as to avoid an argument with Cassandra later; thinking that this may look like a discotheque light show, but at least, and thankfully, there is no thumping bass or irritating DJ trying to wake the dead. If she can force the grenade beneath the outer armour there may be a chance that no one will see the explosion. 'Run. Get away.' Everything about her gestures and expression is screaming this at you, though the words do not escape from between her lips. Cassandra's leg is caught in the tendril grasp of the alien, which is determined not to die alone. A moment more of hesitation will be fatal.

The searing heat of the photon blast rushes over your back, carrying fleshy debris and shards of shell at a vicious velocity. Keeping your face to the ground, you try to screen out the sounds of the splattering fallout, listening for any movement or alarms. As the superheated air cools to a tolerable level, you begin to slide yourself towards the intersection. Looking left, you see the corridor goes on only a short way, culminating at a door with a window in the upper half and a sign below it that reads: Room 204 / Science Lab. Two other doors are opposite each other, between you and the laboratory door. The one on the far wall has the blind down over the window, though it does not obscure the light that is on within. Looking right, you discover the symmetry and three more doorways that complete the exits from this cul-de-sac. It is only that one door that has a light on in the room behind it and you must assume that someone is in there and they are more likely to be hostile than helpful. You stand upright and sneak over to it, keeping your rifle level in one hand and holding out the other, ready to grip the door handle. You can hear singing, possibly a radio set at a volume to be heard clearly within the room, but not beyond it. It is Elvis; one of his early songs. The door suddenly flies open and the deputy head teacher glares angrily at you, with an expression of shock mixed with disappointment and disgust. You escape the forthcoming chastisement by ramming the butt of the gun, hard, into the abdominal region and raising your knee to meet the face.

This is what you came for. Rows of flashing panels, computer screens, oscilloscope displays and radar images giving the appearance of a command centre. The radio sits between a variety of science books upon a shelf above the workbench along the left wall, blaring out an old, distasteful country song, now, about losing the dog, the car, the wife, the kids, the job but, unfortunately, not the will to sing. No one else is in here, though the door in the right wall remains to be investigated. You drag your unconscious former superior inside the room and quietly shut the door. You rummage through pockets and drawers and eventually you find a bunch of keys under a disorganised pile of loose papers on the teacher's desk. It is a huge bunch of keys that form a heavy, metallic mop-head over your fist as you hold them up to inspect them. The teacher's desk will provide a suitable barricade for the time being; a favourable option over testing each key, in turn, in the lock of this door. The other door leads into a storeroom, which is the size of a warehouse. This surprises you as you do not recall the school ever having rooms this large. Weapons and equipment, of all shapes and sizes, are stacked upon shelves, arranged into isles stretching the whole length of the enormous space; a museum display of future technology. You scrutinise a few items, but you can only describe them as 'things from another world' and you cannot even guess as to what purpose they may be intended for. Someone is thumping at the barricaded door. It is someone coming to investigate what the trouble is. It cannot be the deputy head teacher. You know this because the deputy head teacher is still not conscious, moving or making any noise; the wire bindings ripped from the consoles and the chloroform-soaked rag were measures taken to ensure silence and immobility. This is a critical time. You must hold position, in this section, until the second unit arrives.

'No, no, no. You've gotta watch the ball and hit it just as it begins to descend. Poor Winston's knackered from retrieving it, so get it right,' Winston barks in agreement and then limps back to the other side of the line, to sit beside the net and the umpire's chair, 'and, keep your bloody eyes open.'

You bounce the ball a couple of times; turn it in your hand, inspecting the green fluff and white seams for faults and then you throw it way too high in the air.

'No, no, no, no, no. That's way too high, look where it's landed,' the Old Man exclaims with a highly agitated edge to the tone of his voice. He raves on about the technicalities of serving and the manufacturing process of tennis balls, while you watch the flamingos strut slowly over the court. The lurid pink feathers are dazzling in contrast to the deep green of the grass and the wall supporting the scoreboard. Your eyes follow them as they ascend the supporters stands and take their seats in the crowd. 'So, you've gotta get your act together. You're a set down and you haven't won a single point in this one. If you can't play this game, then why did you make this stupid challenge? Here, drink some of this and play your arse off.'

The umpire lifts her sunglasses and peers at her watch. She calls, 'time,' and you march out to the sun-drenched end of the court. A round, freckled face with ginger hair, two arms, two legs and a body attached, holds up a ball in each hand, offering them to you. She frowns and growls, dissuasively, as you reach for the ball in her right hand and smiles the width of her face when you take the one in her left hand. You bounce the ball a couple of times. The umpire interrupts your serve to ask for the people in the bright yellow raincoats to not take photographs with a flash and for the polar bears, in the third row, to move along a little to allow the old lady with the shopping basket to sit down.

Your neighbour has left the wings and teeth in the changing room and is limbering up, on the opposing base line, preparing to return your serve. The ball skims off the grass, millimetres within the line. BLEEP. Your protestations are noted, the decision is overruled and the bleeping machine apologises for the mistake and promises to buy you a drink at the club bar, after the match. Your neighbour stomps across the court, tugging at the tight purple underwear with obvious frustration. Three more aces, the game, and you believe your opponent's undergarments, are definitely shrinking.

The serve is timid, barely halfhearted and the ball plomps by your side to be easily dealt with. You slap it down the line, but your opponent still has room to manoeuvre. Your approach to the net has been anticipated and the ball has been lobbed towards the furthest corner. You scrabble, fall and scrabble again. The attempt is a good one and the point will be awarded. You rush, but cannot run. The ball will land, as it is beyond your reach. You make a desperate dive. A glint in the crowd. A sniper has levelled his gun at you. The shot catches the ball and carries it back over your head as you land heavily on the ground. Turning and standing in one movement you see the ball is about to land your side of the net. You dash back, watching the ball closely as it bounces up, beautifully, to above shoulder height. Your forehand, cross-court smash is hit with such might that it causes the ball to scorch the grass, before speeding off out of reach and into orbit. The spectators are being roused to a state of ecstasy by your sudden revival. They are all on your side, audibly giving their support. They grow louder and louder and more excited with each point you win and you are glad that their irritating hissing, whistling and booing has ceased since your opponent has stopped scoring points. Your neighbour is exhausted, sweat streams down over their forehead and their knees seem, discernibly, wobbly. Match point. You stare at the ball in your adversary's hand. Watch it as it goes into the air. The racket makes contact and sends it, spitefully, at you. FAULT. You ignore the stinging sensation in your left thigh and focus on the ball, again. Bounce, bounce, toss, smash, the ball comes at you a second time. DOUBLE FAULT. Game, set and match ... The crowd roars, hoots, neighs, cheers and applauds and an orchestra of wild antelopes plays a Mozart Concerto in G-flat major using steel drums and a piccolo, all displaying their joy of your triumph.

Darkness. A deep, deep, black darkness; you strain your eyes, but, you still cannot make out anything but darkness. It is not that there is no light illuminating anything, there is just nothing to see. Not even ground. There is nothing below you, nothing above you, nothing to your sides nor to the front or behind you. Nothing, nothing at all. You would call it floating, except that there is nothing around you for you to be floating in. There are no stars, so you cannot liken it to the vacuum of space and there are no walls, so you cannot liken it to being locked in a dark cupboard. You look all around yourself some more, waiting for something to change in the scenery. Finally, you can just make out a white dot, quite some distance away. From it there is a sudden, intense flash that momentarily overloads your senses. Re-opening your eyes you discover that you are, now, surrounded by whiteness. Nothing, nothing but whiteness. It is not that there is too much light to see anything, there is just nothing to see.

AN ALTERNATE LIFE

'Start the engine, Old Man. We're all aboard.'

'Right, oh. Disengage the bloody moorings then.'

Sydney jumps, nimbly, back into the boat, after untying the ropes, and heads forward toward the cabin. He staggers as the engine splutters to life, releasing volcanic like plumes of dark smoke from the exhaust and causing the deck to shudder like an earthquake simulation. Jessica smiles at him, as they squeeze to pass each other in the cabin doorway, and he responds with a serious nod and a feeble, awkward attempt at friendly chit-chat.

The 'Evening Star' chops its course through the gently rolling waves at a fair pace of knots, bringing an extra briskness to the wind upon your face. The land drifts by a few hundred metres to port and you can, clearly, make out people walking amongst the buildings, beyond the beach. The coast seems to stretch on for miles before, abruptly, falling away into the glistening blue sea.

'Care for a glass of wine?' Jessica holds the bottle up, with the label toward you, in one hand and she has two crystal glasses between her fingers in her other hand. 'It's quite good. A light, non-sparkling white. I thought it would be more refreshing, for a day like this, than ice cold lager or warm fizzy cider.'

You take a glass from her and watch the liquid form vast waves in the tiny environment, washing up the sides and collapsing into the centre. She then slides into the seat beside you and, carefully, fills her own glass.

'Ohh, this is, so, wonderful. What an adventure this is turning out to be. Who would have thought I'd be running away, on vacation, with you lot.' Jessica seems to be staring straight at you, into your eyes, but it is difficult to tell through the sunglasses she is wearing. She smiles, warmly, then stretches and sighs, working herself into a relaxed position. Her dark brown hair is sensibly plaited into a long, delicate rope which is left to swing freely behind her. Her blue and white checked blouse is unbuttoned and tied around her body, leaving her stomach exposed, and the almost transparent material of which it is made is appropriate for the warmth of the day. White, pocketless shorts complete her attire, which barely covers any of her slender frame. The sunlight glints off of the base of her glass as she empties the contents and she refills it, after topping up yours. 'Come on, keep up. Only fools do what we're doing sober. Sydney certainly qualifies, but I doubt you do.'

A sailing boat passes to starboard, heading in towards the harbour; the four visible crew members hail greetings and comments about the weather at you until you are out of audible range. Jessica waves enthusiastically and answers them with emphasised civility. She repeats this performance every few minutes and, finally, receives a respite after the 'Evening Star' veers out of the main shipping lanes into the wide, open ocean where only the white pinpoints of distant sails indicates the presence of any other vessels. The land recedes away, like the wake of the boat, eventually dipping over the horizon just as the stars begin to show themselves above it.

'It's so beautiful. I would never have dreamed that it would be as wonderful as this,' Jessica says, stretching her arms above her head and leaning over backwards. She has removed her sunglasses and has placed them on the table beside the empty wine bottle. Her eyes are closed and she inhales deeply; she looks serene in this meditative state. An unexpected area of choppy water makes you instinctively reach out and grab her hand. She grips you tightly and pulls herself back into an upright position. She stares into your eyes briefly and then smiles. 'I'm glad you came along. You're not as quirky as the other two. I like you, I mean, I like you a lot. What do you make of Sydney? He seems a bit weird to me. He always looks at me in an odd way, as though he thinks I'm going to stab him or something. And Captain Venerable is always drunk and an arrogant sod. Well, he comes across that way. I've never seen him sober, so I don't know if that's what he's really like. Come to think of it I haven't known either of them that long, have you?'

She nods politely as you answer her and she pours more wine, from a new bottle, into the glasses and gives short phrases of acknowledgement to what you are saying.

'It's Cassandra you know well isn't it? Yes, I thought so, you work with her don't you? Top secret stuff, eh? Yeah, she was meant to be coming on this trip too, but she's just disappeared. No one seems to know where she is, so we had to leave without her. Do you know what happened to her?'

You watch her expression turn to one of concern while you consider how to deliver the knowledge you possess, most of which you cannot reveal. For what feels like hours she stares at you, patiently awaiting an answer; then, suddenly, her eyes are distracted and they focus, with terror, on something more immediate than the bad news you have to report. Turning around you can see the source of her fear is well founded. What would be normally be described as a UFO, but what you know is actually an alien spacecraft, is approaching the 'Evening Star' at a tremendous velocity. You watch the luminescent, orange blob grow into a fierce, fiery ball against the speckled, black background of the night sky, mesmerised by its implication. The trail it burns through the atmosphere emphasises the hurry they are in to reach you.

'Quick, over the side. Now, come on, trust me.'

Jessica pushes you, indignantly, towards the railing. The waves are dark and uninviting; you can feel them sapping the heat from your body already. Drastic as it may be, this is the only course of action worth considering and you do not have time to come up with an alternative plan. Reluctantly, you ease your legs over and sit atop the railing, pausing to take a deep breath before leaping. You jump, float, splash and then sink. The water is as cold as you expected and when you rise above the surface, again, there is no land in sight for you to head to, so you just swim and watch out for Jessica. You are about thirty metres away from the boat when she bobs up beside you; her hair still flowing, in a single tail, from the back of her head over her left shoulder, unaffected by the sea. She smiles at you and then glances back at the boat. The cabin light is on and you can see figures moving inside.

'I did tell them to abandon ship, but they insisted on finishing their poker game first, so I had to leave without them. Come on. We must get further away from the boat or they might detect us.'

Jessica takes hold of one of your shoulders and turns you in the water, until you are looking up at the sky and at the, nearly here, UFO. Supporting you around the chest with her arms, she swims expertly backwards, rapidly away from the impending doom. She gains more than two-hundred metres of distance between you and the 'Evening Star' before the inevitable happens. The orange blob stops, abruptly, above the tiny boat. Now that it is stationary, you can make out the contours of the craft that define it as a space ship. The colourful glow, emanating from the hull, appears to help keep it in the air; some form of anti-gravity field that is silent and mysterious.

You tread the vast expanse of water, without aid from Jessica, watching the boat bounce beneath the ship waiting for the aliens to act. A hatch is opening in the belly of the spacecraft and a white light erupts out of it to shroud the 'Evening Star' and forcing you to cover your eyes and turn away. When you look back both vessels are gone; only a faint, orange trail leading to a blazing dot amongst the stars provides any evidence to suggest either ever existed.

You shiver, sending a spray of droplets back to where they had come from. An odd, dark shape catches your eye. It rose above the surface and then disappeared again. You feel something brush against you and the water rush around your body.

'Stay still. He won't harm you if he thinks you're dead already. I'll distract him. Don't worry, I'll be back in a minute and you'll be safe,' Jessica says to you before disappearing below the surface, too.

There is a fine line between breathing and drowning when attempting to remain motionless in deep water. You are thankful for the life jacket that magically lifts your head above the waves; even if it is a horrible, lime green colour.

The minutes pass and Jessica, finally, reappears and says apologetically, 'Sorry about that. It was Toby, he's a bit of a bully, but he only seems grumpy when you get to know him. He was just trying to scare you, he knows humans are frightened of him really.' She smiles and then dips out of view to rise the other side of you, splashing you with water. 'He's a shark. A great white, I think. Well, I believe that is what you would call him. Very ferocious when he wants to be. He's a bit pissed off at the moment; an Australian film crew hassled his wife the other day, taunting her with rotten lamb and rusty hooks. I told Toby you weren't Australian and he said it was just as well because he was still full up after devouring two of the film crew, half of their equipment and most of their boat. He was merciful really, he left the diver with the video camera alone.' Amazingly, Jessica is remaining afloat with no apparent movement and without a life jacket; her head stays perfectly above the surface of the sea as she relates the story to you. 'I've sent Toby to get a couple of friends of mine to help us back to shore. They may be a while, though.'

If ever you make it back to shore, you are certain that you will look, feel and move about as much as a prune. Dawn is coming, the sunlight is, slowly, climbing over the distant edge of the planet.

'I love the sunrise, just watching it fills me with energy. It also means bedtime for those bloody aliens. At least we know that they won't be back for a few hours. Can you hear that?'

Jessica asks suddenly distracted.

Yes, you can. It is a strange bubbling noise with a low hum as an undertone.

'Oh no, not them as well. Why can't they all just leave me alone,' Jessica exclaims with dismay. She rises on the swell and dives, head first, under the water. You watch her movement like a slow-motion clip. Watching her legs, or what should be her legs, break above the surface and flip, spraying salty droplets and propelling her speedily down. She did not have legs. Not even a single leg. It was a tail, like that of a fish. A giant fish tail, with red, green, blue and gold scales glistening in the morning light.

The bubbling is louder and the water is vibrating with the hum. The sea is seething, boiling, just to your right about fifty metres away. Something is tugging at your legs and you can feel your life jacket being undone. The straps fall loose and you slip out of it, leaving it bobbing above you as you are dragged down. You desperately hold your breath, but the pressure is building. You know the darkness around you is water rushing before your eyes and there is nothing else, at all, to see. Your lungs are about to explode when the distorted image of Jessica, with weirdly suspended hair, looms up in front of you. You cannot make out the expression on her face, but you guess that she is worried about something. She grips your head in her hands and kisses you, passionately, on the lips, parting them with her tongue. Air is forced into your chest and the fear of drowning out of your mind. Jessica draws away from you and grabs your hands in hers. She looks up to where a long, black, cigar-like shape is easily visible against the dawn lit sea surface. A submarine.

Jessica is pulling at your arm and, with her other hand, she is pointing at another shape moving swiftly toward you. It is a smaller marine vehicle with spear-tipped weapons attached. A blast of bubbles and a whoosh behind your head. Jessica is almost ripping your arm off with the strength that she is dragging you down with, however, you are a dead-weight and neither of you are moving anywhere fast. Another burst of bubbles and Jessica loses her grip. You cannot see her; you turn fully around, look up and down, but she is gone. The marine vehicle is closing in on you to make an easy shot of the kill. One spear-tip remains and you can see your name on it. Ten metres. Six metres. Point-blank, then a sudden redness all around, and something slaps, viciously, against the side of your head. Then everything goes black.

'Careful, careful. You took quite a whack around the face, but, on the other hand, you're lucky to be alive at all. Toby got there just in time to mess that guy up before he shot you. He's sorry that he hit you with his tail when he passed. You've been unconscious for quite a while, so don't worry, your vision will return soon.'

Sure enough, gradually, everything is coming into view through a haze. You focus on Jessica's face, her eyes, her smooth complexion and her smile. She is dry and with legs again. Her right arm is, neatly, bandaged from her wrist to her elbow and she is clothed in a sleeveless, light-yellow summer dress. Looking beyond her, you can see that you are in a cavern expertly decorated and furnished. There is a sofa, two armchairs, a coffee table, two free-standing lamp-stands, a television, four waterscape paintings, two glass-front cabinets, tasteful blue and green carpeting and a bearskin rug on which you are laying. The strangest feature of the room, by far, is the large pond occupying nearly half of the cavern's space. The underwater lighting is spectacular and the plant life around the circumference enhances the effect and then there is the beach area of pure, white sand between the water's edge and the carpeting.

'This is my place. My apartment if you like, it's where I live most of the time. It's secret. I don't have many human visitors, to tell the truth you're the first. The only way in or out is by the lounge lake, as I call it.' As you listen to her words and look over at the little lake you notice Toby's dorsal fin cutting up through the water, appearing like a sail before the wind with no boat attached. 'We're about half a mile below the sea surface, I think, well it's a long swim anyway, and then the nearest land is a tiny island five miles east. Oh look. Toby's come to check that we're all right. Yeah, we're fine thanks, Toby. Don't worry I will. He's always so caring like that. He said he'll warn us if there's any trouble on the way. Anyway, I'll show you around if you're feeling up to it.'

The decor of this cavernous apartment carries an aquatic flavour throughout; blues, greens and yellows are predominant. The first tunnel-like hallway, with its entrance to the left of the bookcase, leads to the bed chambers. You pass two doors, which you are told the bathroom and toilet are behind, and then the hallway splits and offers three choices of direction to head in. Three small tunnel entrances; three small tunnels through which you will have to crawl to reach the bedrooms. Jessica goes into the tunnel to the left, and you get on your hands and knees and take a closer look at the carpet.

You are grateful it is a deep pile carpet, soft and bouncy, and the swirling blue and green pattern with yellow flecks is quite tasteful and interesting.

What appears to be natural daylight pours out from six powerful lamps suspended behind misty panels at the highest point of the domed ceiling. This converted cavern is massive. It comfortably accommodates all the furnishings: the double-bed, wardrobes, dressing table, chests of drawers, bedside tables, lamp-stands and writing desk. The legs and stands are all carved into the shapes of marine animals as are all the handles on the wardrobes and drawers. There are also a few large paintings and several small statues, mostly of dolphins, expertly crafted and probably worth a fortune. The walls have been plastered and then painted blue, shifting shades to a lighter blue and then drifting into pure white towards the misty panels in the ceiling. Potted plants dangle on thin chains at differing heights around the room, providing a surreal underwater effect with the blue walls, marine life ornamentation and sandy yellow carpet. After offering compliments and discussing the difficulties of colour coordination, on hands and knees again you move on to the next bedroom.

The master bedroom is striking. A blaze of cool white, emanating from the ceiling walls and floor. The gigantic white water-bed sits imposing atop a fluffy, white ziggurat, lacy drapes surround it upheld by four tall, gleaming white posts. Mirrors are everywhere, supported in ornate silver frames, reflecting back into the room the light which has no apparent source. The furnishings themselves seem to be illuminating the entire room. Everything is either silver, white or reflective, requiring

a magician to keep it all clean. The furnishings are limited, though: there is only the bed in the middle and numerous mirrors spread about the walls. An opening on the opposite side of this room leads into another, which you presume to be the en suite bathroom and dressing room. 'This room is my favourite,' she tells you, 'I find it easy to relax and worry about nothing when I am in here. It's peaceful and goes on into infinity.' You scrutinise the room in silence for a while, watching yourself being reflected millions and millions and millions of times in the ceiling and all around the walls and beyond, deeper and further than you can see. You are lured into staring, fascinated by the impossible phenomenon and then torn from it by Jessica calling you to follow her. You retreat back to the hallway where Jessica is waiting for you and she says, 'The other bedroom is a junk room, really, and it's in a complete mess. I'll have to show you it some other time.'

The tour of the abode concludes in the kitchen where Jessica begins to prepare a meal. 'Is pasta all right with you? I can make an exciting sauce to go with it, but it will be vegetarian, I'm afraid, and no fish. I find it hard to eat my friends.' She busies herself with various implements and ingredients, chatting away as she does so with no apparent attention being paid to her actual activity. She describes, in detail, the poor state of the seas. The pollution, the shipping, the genocide of marine life and the rising temperatures are all serious matters of concern. And then she elaborates on the situation with the planet as a whole. The alien invasion, the poverty, the disease, politics and everything and then she talks about how she wishes that things were as they were a hundred or so years ago when the silly men in wooden sailing boats used to be terrified of the creatures living in the hidden depths. Nowadays, no one believes in mermaids, let alone the Kraken or the Loch Ness monster. But then, no one believed in aliens either and just look at what's happened; the soulless snail-beasts are everywhere and no one knows where they came from nor how to defeat them.

Jessica ponders for a while. When she speaks, again, she speaks as though she were making a confession, 'Well, that's not strictly true. Some people do believe in mermaids. And they'd like nothing better than to catch me, stuff me and then place me in a glass cabinet, in some ghastly pose, in one of their private museums, beside an exhibit of Dodo and dinosaur eggs. You would have thought that they would want to study me alive, possibly in the wild, but no, they enjoy the chase and especially the kill. I never could understand why humans like killing for fun, even Toby only hunts for food and will kill for protection, and on the odd occasion he has been known to kill for revenge, but never for fun. I'm a pacifist myself. Hurt or be hurt. Take a life or be killed. I would rather it be on their conscience than on mine. The only person you can never run away from is yourself.'

You sit on the surprisingly comfortable pine wood stool leaning over the tiled breakfast bar as you listen to her. The light brown of the cabinets and rusty red of the tiling is quite a contrast from the rest of Jessica's apartment. It is as spacious as any of the other rooms, though it is divided into two areas. A chef's dream kitchen, with all the appliances and plenty of space to move around in, and the other half dedicated to dining with all the appropriate features including candles on the table and a bar offering a generous variety of spirits and wines.

The aroma of well-prepared food begins to fill the air and excite your appetite. You watch her toss the various dishes into an assortment of bowls and then place them neatly on the pine wood dining table, where she directs you to sit. A warmed plate is put before you and you are requested to serve yourself while Jessica lights the candles and opens a bottle of red wine. Mellow jazz guitar music plays, softly, in the background, while you eat and talk. Space, philosophy, religion, history, psychology, physics, neurobiology and the present state of economic affairs in Tunisia; jumping from topic to topic you share ideas and beliefs finding that you have very much in common. Eventually, the conversation turns to Cassandra's demise. Jessica had been a close friend, it is evident in her eyes and trembling lower lip. She dismisses the anxiety by saying, 'Oh well, it was always more than likely to happen considering the profession she was in. Damn those aliens. The moment we're rid of them won't be a moment too soon.'

The cutlery and plates sparkle with cleanliness and are carefully organised back in their cupboards and you now sit beside Jessica on the large sofa overlooking the lounge lake. Her good mood is returning rapidly and she is cheerfully wittering on about the vividness of her dreams and how some of them have been premonitions. She had foreseen the arrival of the aliens and the destruction of the Colosseum in Rome and she is presently telling you her latest dream about the Niagara Falls drying up and the whole of Europe becoming a giant bog. Something to do with the aliens accelerating the global warming process causing the polar caps to melt and flood the planet. The weather would be affected along with the size of the seas and then former deserts would become jungles and lush landscapes, swamps.

You listen to her melodious voice without interrupting, maintaining eye contact so as to show you are paying attention. She stretches occasionally, each time edging nearer to you and now there is physical contact. She has snuggled up to your arm and her head rests on your shoulder, tiredness beginning to show on her angelic, little face. 'Do you dream a lot?' she asks, slowly applying more pressure to your arm as her body relaxes towards limpness. You suspect she is feigning it, attempting to get closer to you. Some of her subtle comments hint that she likes you in an amorous way, which is now being confirmed by her delicate touch and provocative motions. A stray strand of hair tickles your cheek and you react instinctively. Jessica quickly sits up, alarmed by your slight spasm, but her stare of concern returns to one of adoration as you explain your reaction. She kisses you, fully, firmly, moving smoothly to sit astride your lap, her fingers gently caressing your head and shoulders. Passionately, intimately your bodies entwine.

'Toby's calling. Something's wrong.'

You both wriggle out from under the sheets, the water-bed wobbling beneath you, and Jessica runs off to the lounge without bothering to dress. Moments later she is back, insisting that you need not put any more clothes on and that you should hurry because the situation is urgent. She leads you by the hand to the watery exit from the abode, where Toby's dorsal fin can be plainly seen darting back and forth impatiently.

'Quickly, put on the wet-suit while I put the bridle on Toby,' Jessica says to you, pointing at the pile of rubber clothing.

She then dives into the pool with a heap of straps. With wet-suit on you follow her, not entirely without trepidation. The bridle is now secure and the dorsal fin heads toward you with Jessica swimming alongside. She holds up the trapeze like bar and tells you to, 'Hold on tight. Toby will take you somewhere safe, I'll meet up with you later.'

As soon as the bar is in your grasp Toby begins to dive and jerks you deep beneath the surface. Despite the mask protecting your eyes, you cannot see anything for the sheer rush of water created by Toby's tail. Rush, rush, rush, on and on until Toby finally slows and you can see his magnificent form in its full and close up glory. A long, silvery-grey shape, powerful and sleek, at least four times the size of you. His huge flat head swings round; gums, teeth, such teeth and a single, piercing black eye that is visible from this side. This fearsome appearance is dulled only a little by the bridle strapped to his face, giving a vague impression of timidity and tameness. The full light of day ripples over his back, the familiar dorsal fin just penetrating the sea's surface above you. Below is a colourful array of coral, on which Toby almost scrapes his belly. Aware that you have reached your destination and are relatively safe, you let the reins go and you watch Toby majestically swim away, very soon out of sight, slipping back into the darkest depths of the ocean.

The coral reaches up above your waist, so you weave and crunch your way up the slope until it gives way to white sand and your masked head begins to protrude above the gently lapping waves. Through the misty visor you can make out a wide expanse of beach, beyond it the lush, green vegetation indigenous to a tropical island. A welcome and thoroughly deserved haven. Anyone watching from the shore could easily mistake you for a sea-monster rising from the depths to terrorise the islanders. The water drips from the shiny, smooth, black rubber that is making your movements awkward, stiff and clumsy and your flapping, flippered feet leave an inhuman trail in the sand behind you. The tropical heat is imposing and there is soon less water on the outside of the wet-suit than there is within it from the sticky sweat that is creating an adhesive between your own and this second layer of skin. A few metres more and you will be at the tree line and in the shade, where you can sit and peel yourself as you would one of the bananas hanging from some of the tree branches.

Removing the diving suit is quite an endeavour, exhausting and painstaking, but, finally the task is done and all your senses return; sight, smell, hearing and touch one by one as you shed your garment like a snake that has outgrown itself. You eye the fruits of all kinds that dangle amongst the leaves: coconuts, pears, apples, oranges, passion fruit, tomatoes, melons, lemons, strawberries, blackberries, peaches and plums, deciding which ones to take to test your taste buds.

Oh no. You can hear drums, again. A steady, rhythmic beat pounding clearly through the trunks, which add an echoing emphasis of their own. The sound does not instil fear into your heart, though, nor any measure of anxiety. Quite the contrary, you feel a lightness and a desire to dance. It is calypso style and as you strain to listen you can hear the pleasant harmonising of several voices and a selection of string, wind and percussion instruments. It is a happy sound, the noise of a party in progress and you are certain that you can hear laughter and loud chatter. Picking fruit on your way, you head towards the source of the festive sound, a convenient path seems to lead directly to it. In one of the trees you pass, a brightly coloured paradise bird caws at you, 'Looking for the party, looking for the party. That way.' It points, with one wing spread, down the path you are already on. 'That way. Keep going, keep going.'

The music gets louder and louder and you can see a large, crowded clearing opening up before you, the noise of people enjoying themselves is quite discernible now. Two people, suddenly, come running up the path and push by you, heading into the bushes. The male shouts an apology for bumping you and then disappears into the undergrowth with the giggling female. In the strength of the sun, again, and amongst hundreds of bouncing bodies, you are enveloped by the electric atmosphere and cannot keep yourself from dancing, wiggling your butt and waving your arms with the rest of them. You are passed drink after iced drink and welcomed excitedly by everyone that looks at you. Some of the faces you recognise; that woman there, in the red bikini, you have seen her on television reading the evening news and the man in the yellow shirt with blue pineapples on it is, certainly, that nasty politician, whose name escapes you.

The musicians are a fair way off, above and beyond the crowded clearing, which appears not to be a clearing at all, but a huge garden surrounded by tropical trees. Over the heads, hats and parasols you see a mansion, with golden bricks, stained glass windows, statues and all, spreading as wide and high as the garden is long. A truly massive building. The surging sea of people breaks at its steps. At the top of the steps, in between the columns, is the band jumping and dancing to the music they are making; a funky, disco sort of sound at the moment. Aretha Franklin and James Brown are doing a duet and you would swear that it is Louis Armstrong playing the trumpet in the third row.

Someone is calling your name, preceded by Captain, over and over. A man in a military uniform is strutting over to you from one of the tents serving drinks. 'Captain, I am sorry to trouble you. I am Lieutenant Carter and I have been sent to collect you for an urgent mission. We were informed that you were here by a Miss Jessica, who swam up alongside our aircraft carrier just offshore of this island. She disappeared before any of the officers could lean over the side to talk to her and it was some time before we were convinced by the gunner that a mermaid had spoken to him. We thought he was drunk. It was the Commander who recognised your name and he wishes to see you immediately. I do regret having to take you away from such an excellent party, but the helicopter is waiting.'

TO UNSEEN PLACES

The Commander sits in his familiar position, in his huge chair, looking out of the sloping windows, watching the aircraft launches and the teams of technicians loading their weaponry. You step into the room and salute at the rear of his head. To the left of his desk sits another man in another huge chair. He is regal, you can tell by the long, red cloak, sceptre and slightly squashed crown upon his brow. His face, behind the silvery-grey beard, is stern, betraying his attempts to conceal his concern.

'At ease, Captain. This is King Berthold IX, you may have met,' the Commander's voice booms back off the glass and you answer that you have not been formally introduced. The King swaps his sceptre to his other hand and shakes yours briskly and then sits down, again. The Commander resumes the briefing, 'I am cutting short your leave for a very delicate assignment. The King, here, has discovered the alien base on Earth near the northern border of his country. He also thinks that it is a prison camp holding several of his citizens and maybe some of ours. I want you to accompany His Highness' rescue party and disable the radar system that they've got there, then we can send in reinforcements. I don't want to lose any more aircraft, that bastard Melcroft at HQ is after my job and any more bad reports will ruin me. See to it, Captain.

I need that base destroyed, I mean humankind needs that base destroyed. This operation is bound to be shown on TV worldwide, I've got reporters embedded in my arse. Damn press, they make the whole war seem unreal, just like a bloody sci-fi movie. People love their explosions and violence. They'd feel differently if they were here. You will leave with the King in ten minutes. Carter will be your pilot, he is waiting for you in launch bay seven.'

From outside, you can hear cries of clear the deck and only a few seconds later an almighty explosion blasts against the window, forcing the panes to wobble, the walls to shudder and the deck to tremor. The Commander is swearing immodestly about the loss of another aircraft and King Berthold is matching his coarseness with comments about the state of his crown that has slipped from his head and rolled under a stack of falling books. Wispy holes appear in the smoke and it is plain to see that the damage is much more extensive than just the loss of one aircraft. A hole, half the deck across and penetrating over two decks down, has been gauged out of the end of the runway platform. A bomb must have come loose during a take-off. The Commander launches into a fresh deluge of shameless expletives, increasing in volume and vulgarity, at the sight. Between curses you are dismissed and the King follows you out in an obvious hurry to be off the ship.

Men, in blue life-jackets, are dashing about the passageways in a flow that is perpetually against you, alarms and flashing red lights are everywhere reflecting from the metal walls, ceiling and floor, adding to the general chaos and confusion. Over the shouting and stamping you can hear the terrifying creaking noise. The noise is familiar from all the

Titanic movies you've watched; the ship is ripping apart and sinking. You have no idea where you are going and the King has no more idea than you. He orders a running man to stop and is completely ignored. The next person receives a knee to the stomach and an elbow in the neck before the King politely asks him to stop and give him directions to bay seven. The King thunders off, pushing everyone out of his way with indignation and you chase after him, leaving the groaning sailor to his pitying mates. That noise, the breaking ship noise, is louder and stronger and the corridor is contorting and twisting ahead of you and you are being thrown about like a pair of knickers in a tumble dryer.

King Berthold has taken a turn at the junction, but upon reaching it you cannot tell which way he went. You stumble left with the sudden lurching roll of the ship and fall through a hard, metal door into the open launch bay, which is sloping at thirty degrees to the horizon. You roll some more, away from the helicopter which has just taken-off because of the unstable platform. You thump into the far wall of the bay and stare up into the open sky. The helicopter is hovering, holding position above the carrier waiting for you to get nearer to it. You try to scrabble and climb up the steep gradient of deck plates, but you cannot get a good hold and your progress is painfully slow. A deep screech, deafening, sustained. The floor tilts up further and you catch your chin on a plate edge as you slide down into water. You are up to your waist in seawater and the ship is disappearing from all around you. The helicopter cannot get near enough, there is nothing they can do.

A red blob has dropped out, a life jacket? It is plummeting fast and on target for you. It is too big to be a life jacket, maybe it's a raft. No, rafts do not normally scream like that nor do they have limbs that flap around wildly. The immense G-force effect as you are plucked from the water is almost enough to knock you out. The bungee cord is pulling you and the King back up towards the helicopter and as the world stops spinning you look down and watch the last few metres of aircraft carrier go bubbling under. Little white boats and orange inflatable rafts are bobbing to the nearby shore of the island, where you can see the party is still going on. Thankfully, the bungee is losing its bounce and you no longer feel like a giant yo-yo being played with a mile above the Earth's surface.

'Carter's the only one up there and he's flying the vessel. You climb up first, Captain,' shouts the King into your ear. The wind is blowing hard and you've got a long way to climb. The wind, with droplets of icy water, stings your exposed skin as it hits you and pushes you from side to side, your mass acting as the weight to a pendulum. The rubbery cord is slippery and whips about in your wind frozen grasp. Hand over hand you stretch up and up towards the awaiting hovering box, compelled by King Berthold shouting encouragement from below, 'Carry on, doing well, almost there.'

A violent, icy blast of wind almost sends you flying just as you are pulling yourself into the belly of the helicopter, and just at the moment you catch sight of the parachutes on the opposite side, next to the closed door. A timely shove from the King saves you and he springs inside after you as though the craft were still on the ground. He then leans back out, again, and hoists the bungee cord in, laying it in a neat coil in the corner.

'All aboard?' comes a shout from the cockpit.

'Yes,' King Berthold shouts back in a strained voice. He is struggling to pull the door closed, stretching out, with all limbs in an 'X' shape, gripping the door in one fist and the frame in the other, his red cloak swishing about him in heroic fashion. '-ing, -ing door.' The swearing continues until the door is shut. He then returns to shouting at the cockpit, 'Yes, we are all aboard. Now, take me home, I need a bath.' With these, his last words directed to anyone in particular, he sits down and begins to examine his crown, crying out the occasional obscenity about the state of it.

Carter's mood is no better. This is the fourth aircraft carrier that had been lost during this war with the aliens, three of them accidents. The carrier which the aliens captured had been abandoned by her crew when the enemy was first sighted. The odds were estimated at 2051 to 1 against at the start of the war. Earth doesn't have technology that can even match that of the aliens, the odds now have nine digits one side and one the other, not in Earth's favour, of course. Then Carter goes on about the ineptitude of the generals and the politicians, explaining that if more money was put into space programs and planetary defence instead of peoples' back pockets we would be winning this war. His criticism knows no end; he goes on into detail about blundering military tactics and the number of lost ships, aircraft, personnel and satellites. Even the International Space Station had been captured. The generals and scientists are still puzzling over how the aliens are managing to operate it, considering they are too large to move about any section of it. 'The moon will be next,' he exclaims in disgust.

The helicopter enters a patch of choppy air and Carter's immediate attention is drawn to the controls. Suddenly, every panel is flashing, sending out a code that could only mean distress.

'Oh shit. Oh bugger, oh ...'

'What!? What is it, what's wrong now?' screams the King as he forces his head and shoulders through the cockpit doorway.

'I'm sorry, Your Highness, but, I forgot about the radar base on the border of your country. We have been detected and an alien spacecraft will intercept us in thirty-seven seconds, thirty-five, four, three, oh shit, oh ...'

'Well, we'll have to jump for it then. Free-fall for a while, so as to remain unnoticed by our alien friends, and then open up the parachutes at the last minute, hoping that we land my side of the border. Any one of my subjects will help us get back to my palace.' The King withdraws from the doorway.

'Oh shit, twenty-five, four, three, oh shit, ohh ...'

'Come on, come on,' hollers the King. He looks at you harshly as you step into the windy compartment, the door is open, ready for your departure. King Berthold straps you up tightly and tells you to pull the cord after a count of twenty. Don't forget because it is a close thing. With a shove, you are floating. Floating in a particularly downward fashion. The Earth spreads out beneath you, an unmarked map with patches of dark green, yellow, brown and grey, with the odd dab of blue. It is a living painting, seen from this height, so distant and untouchable, yet real and within reach. As you stare down, closely into each detail, you can begin to make out rivers and fields, groups of buildings and roads, piles of hay and individual horses. Hey, aren't you counting? You jerk the cord and feel the cloth jump from the bag and flutter up above you, opening up like a genetically engineered, fast-growing flower. You feel the sharp tug of the parachute, only momentarily, before the sharp smack of the ground.

'A'e yo' alri't?' a quaint farmer, who is leaning over you, asks. His tone of voice suggests that he doesn't really care, or maybe it's the thick accent. An accent which you couldn't even guess at the origin. 'Yo've land on my 'orse,' he says, 'I 'ope yo' 'aven't kill 'er. 'urry oop ' n' untankle yo'self so I can see ift 'e's 'urt.' Under his breath he mutters, 'Bloody foreigners, droppin' oot sky now. T'is tourist trade tain't bloody wort' it. I'd tell t' King ift ever I'd see 'im. Tell 'im just wot I t'ink of 'is foreigners.' He nudges you aside and kneels beside his horse's head, patting it gently on the neck and softly saying, 'Tremighan. Tremi, wake oop. A'e yo' bre'thin'? Tremighan, wakey, wakey. Well I can see 'e's alive, 'er legs a'e movin'. I'll go 't guy 'ho calls 'imself a vetranaryhan. Yo' stay 'n' look a'ter my 'orse, 'til I'm back.'

You stare at the horse, still twitching under the rope and cloth of the parachute, only its head and two front hooves are exposed. A beautiful, great animal, silky black with a silvery mane. You notice two strange grey bumps on either side of its forehead, resembling small horns. Steam, or is it smoke, puffs out from its nostrils. A clap of thunder in the distance. Not thunder but the destruction of the helicopter. A neigh, shudder and one last puff of smoke. The horse is inanimate. There is a chill in the air and night is coming on surprisingly quickly. You look down at the horse again and see that the parachute has glided across to cover the horse like a shroud. The cord applies itself with impossible zeal, it is possessed, whirling around the horse's body, binding it up to resemble mummification. The gusts of wind are forcing you back. Straw and dust form a swirling cloud obscuring the deceased beast from view. A mushroom of flame and the display is all over and daylight returns to the sky. The ground in front of the stable is bare, the horse and parachute are gone.

There is a disturbance in the trees, behind you, beyond the muddy trail that leads into this stable yard. You swivel round to see something crashing through the branches, wailing in terror and pain over the sound of snapping wood.

'Mind out below,' comes a shout from above. King Berthold IX is gracefully gliding down to where you are standing and you step aside to let him land. A perfect landing, knees bent and a little run to finish. Carter crawls out of the bushes, a bundle of twigs, leaves and cordage, looking like he has had a shabby attempt at camouflage. He staggers into the yard and stands stiffly to attention, salutes to the King and then to you. He politely says, 'Well done, Your Highness. A very fine landing. As skilled a landing as any of our elite paratroopers.'

'Yes, thank you, Lieutenant Carter. Bad luck landing in the trees for you, but we all seem to be in one piece. Quite exhilarating that, may have to try it again someday, when there aren't any aliens about. Right now, our priority is to get back to the palace and for that we will need horses. We don't have any of that new technological stuff here, you know. Oh no, we prefer the old ways. Ah, there's a couple of chaps who will help us,' the King turns to holler at the two men approaching from the house. 'You there. I require your services.'

'Wot 'ave yo' don wit' my 'orse?' the farmer inquires angrily, staring at the blank patch of ground where the horse had lain injured. He is completely baffled and ignores the King's demands for him to pay attention. He looks all round the yard, in the stable, behind it and out into the trees and surrounding fields until he is grabbed roughly by the arms, shaken and told that he will pay attention or he will lose his head. 'Where's my 'orse?' the farmer repeats, still befuddled by its disappearance. 'Yo' were lookin' a'ter 'er,' he says to you. 'Wot yo' don wit' 'er?'

'Answer me,' screams the King with such ferocity that his crown leaps from his head to land, softly, in a steaming pile of manure. The redness, expression and throbbing veins in his forehead tells you that he is nothing less than livid. His carrying voice with its ruthless rhetoric and diabolical threats is heard by all the farmers in their homes for a twelve mile radius. By the time he calms down and is shouting at a normal volume, a small gathering has formed outside the fencing around the yard. Sensing that he now has an audience, King Berthold IX returns to the point. 'You are a subject of my realm and it is my duty to protect you, your family and your land from our enemies. Your duty is to support your king and do as he wishes. I am your king and I require three horses so that I may return to my palace and organise my forces with our allies here. You will be so good as to provide this transportation for me, right now.'

'But, but, I can't 'elp yo', me liege,' the farmer whimpers, 'Yo' foreigner, ally friend 'ere 'as stolen 'er, 'idden 'er. Fell from t' sky 'n' flatten 'er 'ee did. Me only 'orse.' He waggles his finger at you. 'Wot yo' don wit Tremighan? Wot yo' don wit' my 'orse?'

The farmers, who have come from the nearby houses, have started chatting amongst themselves speculating what might have happened here. They fall into silence when the King speaks to address them all.

'I am King Berthold the Ninth, your ruler. I want you all to go and get your horses, bring them here and I will choose the three best mounts.'

The crowd stares at him mutely, not stirring an inch. One asks a farmer next to him, in a whisper, 'I dunno, do yo' t'ink 'e's really t' King?'

The whispered answer, 'I dunno, 'e 'asn't got 'is crown on. Our good King Berthold always wears 'is crown.' This observation receives approving nods from the other farmers who were near enough to hear it.

King Berthold IX also heard the comment and understood the truth of it. He is livid, again, and screams out, 'It's there,' pointing with his finger, 'there, there in the middle of that pile of dung. You see, it's there. My poor crown, it's filthy. Now, get me some bloody horses.'

The group of thoroughly convinced farmers disperse to carry out their king's order, leaving only the original farmer, who is still asking what you have done with his horse, and the timid veterinarian.

'Do you want me to knock him out for you, sir?' Lieutenant Carter asks you in earnest, but before you can answer him the King has already grabbed and begun interrogating him about the subject.

The farmer repeats his story about how you fell out of the sky and landed on his only horse, of him going to get the vet leaving you to keep an eye on his only horse and on his return his only horse is gone and instead his king is here wanting a horse, and he shouts accusations, at the end of his statement, that not only are you a bloody foreigner but a bloody witch too. The King goes to say something in your defence, but the farmer just carries on over him telling about how he raised the horse from a foal, a lost and lonely foal he had found wandering in the woods, weak and starving. She was bad tempered and hated working, but he loved that horse, it was his only friend. Nothing could replace his Tremighan, they were going to do great things together, they were going to win the Derby and other races and earn a fortune in prize money. The farmer is about to go into what they were planning on doing with the money when King Berthold IX cuts him off with a promise to give him a fortune and a herd of horses and then strides over to the open gate to meet the other farmers returning with the transportation.

A misshapen cart, with wheels more square than circular, is dragged, creaking and shuddering, into the yard by a grey, very miserable looking donkey. Next come two elephant sized mares of the Shire variety, brown with beige hair covering their hooves and providing a hippie-style mane. After them follows another donkey, a fidgety beast, then a large dog, a goat, a pig, three chickens and a giraffe. The King is disappointed to say the least. He doesn't even swear at the farmers who are lined up, standing proudly in front of their animals. He walks along the line as though it is an inspection, but the choices are already obvious. One of the Shire horses is lame and is having difficulty standing on two legs, the other is a little too flatulent to accompany the King's party. It is just ridiculous to think about riding the other animals, so, the two donkeys and the rickety cart it is; though the King does consider having a saddle and bridle put onto the giraffe.

'Quickly, now. Load enough provisions for us to get to town and prepare this animal,' the King prods the fidgety donkey, 'for me to ride. And someone retrieve and clean my crown.'

Eventually, you are underway. Lieutenant Carter has the reins and you are squeezed in beside him. King Berthold IX rides alongside cursing the beast he is riding for making him grip his crown so tightly. You are jolted, pounded and crushed and soon have to take over the reins to allow Carter to freely retch over the side. The King manoeuvres his donkey to your side of the cart and strikes up conversation with you to distract himself from the pitiful display beside you.

'So, what is your version of the incident?' he asks in a compassionate and authoritative tone. You tell him your side of the story, but it is a while before the King responds. 'The horse's name was Tremighan, was it not? Hmm, that may not be good. It is bad luck in our country to kill a horse with a name like that. Yes-s-s. Very, very bad luck indeed. You see when a new foal is born the mother has the right to choose whatever name she wishes in their own equine tongue. The name is then changed into our language and then we jumble the letters up to create a different name. We do this because most of the horses' names can have an influence on their behaviour and we do not want to encourage them any further than their own kind already do. The worst bit is that the horses translate for us and of course they may be lying about their names, but we will never know because no human has ever learned Equine. The horses seem to have a pact between them from birth that they will never teach a human their language.' The King pauses a moment as though waiting for you to say something and then answers a question you did not ask. 'Yes, it is very strange that the horses were able to figure out our speech and yet we cannot fathom theirs. However, they did tell us it is because we tend to point at the things we talk about and make gestures for the ones we cannot directly see. Horses do not point at anything and their gestures are too subtle to notice what they mean. Nightmare, eh! A horse named Nightmare. Quite, terrifying. It is said that a horse of that name will haunt you for the rest of your life, follow you everywhere and catch you, when you are alone outdoors at night. It will take you to an unpleasant place of horror, against your wishes, within the blink of an eye. Let us hope we will reach a town before nightfall. We should make it if this infernal cart stays together.'

This is doubtful; already the wheel between you and the King is flopping from side to side in an odd weaving pattern through the ruts and rocks in the path. You are taking it slowly and carefully, at such a pace that it would probably be better to walk. Over hills and grazed pasture, through ploughed fields and bubbling brooks you progress towards a town that the King insists is there. The failing light is adding to his agitation, along with the moans from Carter and the fidgeting of the donkey he is riding. He has gone a little way ahead and you can see his silhouette atop the next hill. It is a graceful, almost ballet-like posture. His right arm up curving over his head to hold on his crown. His left arm curving to his waist, holding the reins and the donkey's mane tightly, so as not to fall himself. His knees bent outward around the barrel belly of the beast, rigid and toes pointed deep into the stirrups.

'Hurry along, there,' he hollers back at you. 'There's an

inn up ahead. We can stop there for the night and send a messenger onto the palace.'

As soon as you 'gee' on the donkey you realise it was a mistake. You pitch sideways and tumble off the path into the field of tall grass amidst broken bits of wheel. Carter is face down on the path, retching again, and the donkey is continuing up the hillside as though nothing was amiss, but grateful for the lightening of the load. The pieces of wood scattered along the path are not recognisable as a cart anymore and Carter is in no shape to walk. You go over and attempt to help him up, but he is too wretched and you will have to carry him. The King has disappeared over the hilltop and the donkey appears to be in no mood to turn back, so you heave Carter over your shoulders and begin to stagger towards the promised inn. The hilltop glows with the last rays of the sun, which is setting far, far beyond it. Each step is shorter and each breath is harder and the inn in is still not in sight. It is almost too dark to see. The stars' blaze, as they may, do not strike the Earth with much effect from such a distance. The moon is reluctant to rise and the sun has now set. Darkness prevails.

You can hear the rustling of crops in the breeze either side of you and the heavy thumps of feet hitting the ground below you. These are discernible sounds that have definite location, but you cannot tell where the galloping noise is coming from. Ahead? Behind? You quicken your pace and just hope it is King Berthold IX returning to you with fresh horses. Step after step after step after step, each one you feel will be your last, Carter pressing on your aching neck. You slip on the unseen edge of the path, grazing your knees on the sharp stones, you stand and stagger on. The galloping has slowed to a trot and it is definitely behind you. Upon reaching the hilltop, you can see the lights of the inn, resting peacefully in the valley below. You run and stumble down the hill, keeping just ahead of the steady clapping of horse hooves. You can even hear its breath. There is, also, a faint smell of burning. Burning flesh. The ground gives way and as you fall you catch a glimpse of your stalker. A huge, magnificent animal. Black with a silvery mane and fiery red eyes. Two grey horns protrude from its forehead and black, leathery wings spread out from its sides.

You are up and running, leaving Carter groaning in the mud. You will send someone to get him once you are inside the inn. The trotting persists behind you, pushing you along. Through the windows you can see people moving and you can hear the hum of conversation and laughter from within the building. However, the entrance to the establishment is not where it should be. There are steps up to where a door would normally be and a frame for it to fit in, but instead of a door it is just a blank wall, no handles, no latches, no hinges, no locks, no nothing, just a wall. You reach the steps and then run over to a window, bashing on it to gain attention. No one within notices. You hammer harder and harder feeling that the glass should break. It does not and still no one hears you.

You feel a smoky breath come over your shoulder. Run. Around the inn, through the stable, over the fence into the backyard. Same again; steps, door frame, no door, more wall. Run. Over the next fence, through a gate, around the side of the building. You bash more windows to no avail, every window you pass. Keep moving. The front of the inn, again, no steps, no windows, but a door. A door. You run to it, turn the handle and push.

A blinding whiteness. The light is too bright and it is a moment before your eyes adjust. Large, single-glaze, wooden frame windows are directly in front of you, the sun blazes in through them at such an angle as to catch every reflective surface. The chromium-plated sink and sideboard glare fiercely beneath the wide window, to the right and to the left are smaller windows and another is set in a yellow painted door. A back door, which opens to wooden steps leading down into a shadowy, enclosed garden, the wooden fencing around it reaching up as high these first-floor windows.

In the sink is a bottle of washing-up liquid, on its side, with water streaming over it from the tap above. On the sideboard is a single, yellow saucer, smashed into three, jagged pieces and tiny, dusty fragments. The cup lies in the same condition on the yellow vinyl covered floor. The broad fronts of the cupboards and drawers are yellow, broken by a thin chrome strip along the top edges. The glossy cupboards spread out along the wall to your right, above and below the white, laminated work surface upon which dozens of clean, white plates are shattered, the shiny silver of the cutlery twinkle like nuggets in a pile of white, powdery stone.

Turning fully around, the huge mirror is immediately visible, a chaotic mosaic distorting the reflection of the window and door. What was used to smash the mirror is on the floor, below it, in a pool of blood. The carving knife stands upright in the last of multiple wounds in her chest and abdomen. You cannot see her face, matted, brown hair conceals it. She is not moving, not breathing, but blood still oozes from the punctures. She has not been dead long.

You notice smudged, red footsteps leading away from the

body, through the doorway to the next room. The door is shut. You cannot tell where the footprints go from there, but you can see that they returned. The trail leads back to you. Blood is on your shoes and on your clothing.

The telephone is ringing. The tap is running. Outside children are laughing. The doorbell chimes, and moments later chimes again. A knock, and again, then the doorbell, telephone, laughter all the time the constant flow of water drumming on the plastic bottle. A fist now pounds at the door, one, two, three. One, two, three. The ringing stops, the pounding stops, the laughter breaks into tears. A child is hurt. The tap runs on. A new sound. Jangling metal. A key slides into the lock of the front door. Footsteps, in the other room. A female voice calls out, 'Janice. Janice, are you up?' The footsteps fade away and then return, 'Oh, my god!' growing louder. 'Oh no. No, no. What's happened? Janice, Janice?' approaching the kitchen. The handle turns and the door opens.

'Ah, there you are. I was beginning to worry about you.' The King sets down his mug of beer and comes over to slap his hand on your shoulder, he then says, 'Where have you left Lieutenant Carter? I'll send someone to get him.' He screams at the barkeeper to organise a search party and then he helps you into a seat by the fireplace. One of the bark covered logs snaps, sending a shower of sparks onto the flagstone floor, the flames dance over the newly exposed area of unburned wood and a wave of heat surges into the room.

It is a large room with plenty of people in it. Some stand by the bar, others sit upon wooden benches at wooden tables and a few are wandering around searching for the toilets. There is an atmosphere of merriment, the music is performed by the prancing troubadour, who now has two accomplices with him and the service is provided by four rather butch and hairy barmaids.

'Would you care for a drink, Captain? Whisky? They concoct their own around these parts, lacks a little in flavour, but it bloody well makes up for it in potency. It'll certainly warm you up and calm you down,' the King says before screaming out for attention, 'Service. Give me some bloody service over here.' An eye-blink later, all four barmaids are gathered around his chair waiting to take his order. 'One whisky and hurry up.'

In the seconds it takes for your drink to arrive, the search party returns and King Berthold IX strides over to see that Carter is attended to and all the baggage collected together. You stare into your drink that has been placed on the round table beside you. The small glass contains a measure of lime green, bubbling liquid. A misty vapour rises up and pours over the edge of the glass, it looks too hot to touch and it releases an aroma like that of a steaming compost heap. Mighty flames roar up the chimney; the whisky is as volatile as it is potent. A barmaid comes over to you and asks whether you would prefer something else. You hand her the glass and reorder. In a gruff tone she asks, 'Would like fries with that?' and then heads off to the bar.

The flames in the fireplace have died down and everyone returns to the conversations they were having before the distraction. You listen to them impartially as you look about your surroundings, noticing the brass pans and animal heads hanging from the beams and the curious new video game in the corner. A couple of adventurers, at a nearby table, are discussing the creature that lives in the castle on the cliff further to north. They are planning to infiltrate the castle and kill the beast during daylight. During daylight was where the agreement ended.

'You can't seriously think that oversized splinter is going to kill it, do you? And I suppose you expect me to hold the damn creature down while you hammer it into its heart, ha! I don't intend to get that close.'

'So, what do you suggest then, Melbrik? A silver sword, a poisonous weed, holy water?'

'No, Subren, I don't. Someone told me the best thing would be a flamethrower.'

'And where do you expect us to get one of them!? Doldor the blacksmith won't know what you're talking about, he'd laugh and tell you to go find a magician. A flamethrower! You're so gullible, Melbrik and stupid. Why I teamed up with you I don't know.'

'If you don't like me then deal with the creature by yourself or find someone else stupid enough to go with you. I think it's stupid wanting to get that close to the damn thing.'

'You're calling me stupid! You, Melbrik, are calling me, Subren, stupid. At least I can spell my name and I can read the sign that tells me the right toilet to go into.'

'Well, I'm not the one who had to chase my horse all the way home because I said *let's go* before I got on, was I, Sooobren. I am always having to tell you to be careful with what you say around them, but you won't listen to me will you, oh no. And then you cry about how you don't realise, for days and days and days. Boo hoo, boo hoo, boo hoo!'

'You bastard, Melbrik. Anyone can make that mistake—'

'No they couldn't. Only you. You remember that time you told your horse to wait for you, but you didn't say where and you found it waiting in a meadow three leagues away, ha ha, ha ha. Or that time when you stubbed your toe on the tethering post and said shit. Oh that was funny, that one ...'

The argument continues, general insults are traded, many other subjects are brought up, but the creature is no longer the centre of their debate. Your attention is distracted by a bare-chested man in a kilt, who is leaning over your shoulder breathing the vile smell of steaming compost down your neck.

'D'ye believe me?' he asks in a strong Scottish accent. He holds up a chainsaw, threatening to pull the cord to start it up. 'My gre't, gre't gran'father found that key and it's my birthri't. No one can 'ave it but me, not even those snivellin' aliens. I'll chop 'em int' bits before they get their slimy tentacles on it.' He pulls the cord, hard, and the chainsaw buzzes into life, inches from your face. He waves it around your head and shouts out his name and something about a fair fight, but you cannot quite hear him. Two of the barmaids have run over and are wrestling Conner MacDonald for the chainsaw. They wrench it from his grasp and beat him to the ground. The chainsaw is silenced and returned to him with a warning not to start it up again, because the other customers found the noise and fumes offensive. He groans and asks them to order him a taxi. The barmaids ignore him as they are now engaged in breaking up the fight between the two adventurers.

You sit back and take a sip of your re-ordered drink, staring into the fire, again, listening to the dirge of the troubadours who have continued playing and singing throughout the excitement. The song seems to be about the love of a lady, the laughter of children and the falling of conkers in the autumn. The lyre, accordion and warbling voice create an irritating and profoundly unpleasant noise. The only tips they receive are to, 'go home', 'shut up', or just plain, 'die will you!'

'Sorry to leave you like that, Captain,' apologises the King on his return. 'Carter's all tucked up in bed and a messenger has been sent. Our escort should arrive by morning, it's not too far to the palace. I think I'll turn in myself, now. It's been a rather exhausting day, what with the ship sinking, us diving out of the helicopter and that horrible business with the farmers.' He yawns. 'Oh, I must remember to get the jeweller to see to my crown. Good night, Captain.' He rises from his seat then turns to say, 'The barkeeper will show you to your room when you are ready and he will fetch you when it is time to get up. See you in the morning.' He strides off to the stairs leading up to the bedrooms, his immaculate, red cloak trailing out heroically behind him.

Conner MacDonald is up and limping to the door, having been told to wait outside for a carriage which will take him to the nearest gutter. The barmaid then comes to you and asks if there is anything else that you want. You are about to say something when she turns and walks away as though you had already answered. You swallow the last of your drink and then head in the same direction as the King.

The short, red faced, white-haired barkeeper intercepts you at the bottom of the stairs and in the same rich accent of the farmers he says to you, 'Yo' want t' go t' bed? I'll show yo' t' way.' He steps behind the bar and brings back a lantern and a set of keys. 'Yo' be needin' t'ese,' he says, shaking them about in front of you. He then slowly ascends the stairs muttering something about the awful behaviour of the clientele and the smell they leave behind them.

Each step creaks in protest of the weight put upon them and the banister wobbles in sympathy for their strain. The floorboards of the landing are in no better condition and there is a faint smell of damp and rot. The barkeeper, holding the lantern high, turns to check that you are still following and sighs as though disappointed when he sees that you are. Stopping, abruptly, in front of one of the doors on the left he turns to you again and inquires, 'Is t'at yo' 'orse waitin' outside? T' one wit' wings. 't is in a mighty foul temper 'n' won't stay in t' stable. 'ere yo' are, I 'ope yo' find 't comf'table. Good night.' He hands you the keys and lantern and then shuffles, slowly, back down the landing muttering something about the crudeness of the customers and the state they leave the rooms in.

The room is very comfortable, for the rats and cockroaches that is. The bed is a plank of wood, two feet wide with a coarse, brown blanket thrown over it and the curtain is a dirty, moth-eaten rag nailed up over the hole in the wall pretending to be a window. The floorboards creak as much as the stairs and you can, clearly, see the rot and mould, which is the closest thing to decoration that the room exhibits. The lantern you are holding is the only source of illumination.

Something falls from the ceiling onto your shoulder, its legs kicking about desperately trying to get a hold. Another bounces off of your head and tumbles to the floor in front of you, where it is immediately set upon by two large, brown rats, their teeth sinking into the bulbous abdomen and head simultaneously. The rats tear it apart, mercilessly, spraying yellow, pussy life fluid and eight long, black, hairy legs all around the room. The arachnid on your shoulder has a grip and is heading for the relative safety of your collar; the long, black legs probe around your neck and right ear. Reflexively, you sweep it away with the bunch of keys in your hand and step away from it as it lands and is assaulted by three more rats that have come scampering from beneath the bed. You look up to see what else might drop on you. The ceiling is crawling. It is a mass of crawling creatures, the largest of their kind, climbing over each other in one, black, writhing mass, disguising the true colour and texture of the ceiling. You recoil back out of the doorway, along the landing, down the stairs and straight to the bar where you order a whisky to calm your nerves.

'T' room not t' yo' likin'?' the barkeeper asks as he passes you the glassful of steaming, green liquid. You tell him that you are cold and would prefer to sit by the fire until morning.

The morning is cold, the sky hangs low and grey. Rain has fallen during the night leaving the ground soggy, the roads like rivers of mud and the fauna drooping, listlessly, with the weight of the icy water. Four strong horses lead a large, golden carriage up the path to the door of the inn; eight well-armed cavalry men before and eight after, providing an impressive regal escort, steam rising from all of them forming an ominous cloud that follows above the procession. Still by the fireside, you watch them, through the four-paned window by the door as they pull up.

A mug is placed on the table beside you by the barkeeper,

who says, 'Mornin' t' yo'. Fine day eh? T' King will be down in a mo'.' Thump, creak, thump, creak, thump, creak a few strides and King Berthold IX flops into the seat on the other side of the table. He sighs, looks at you and then leans forward preparing himself to say something awful.

'Got some bad news for you, Captain, I'm sorry to say. It seems that Carter was got at by a poisonous spider last night and is lying stiff as a board, this morning. Either that or he's a very difficult man to wake. However, it appears that we will be going on to the palace without him as we do not have a minute to lose. Barkeeper,' he shouts aloud, 'Barkeeper, bring me a bloody coffee. And make it strong, strong I say.' He settles back in the chair and looks out of the same window you have been. 'Ah, good. My guards have arrived. We will be off as soon as I've finished my cup.'

The barkeeper rushes over and offers a huge, ornate mug resting on a sparkling, silver tray to the King, keeping his head bowed low and mumbling words that are appropriate when in the presence of royalty. He then shuffles off, just as quickly, once the King is holding the mug firmly in his hands, muttering something about the class of the patrons and how they always give insultingly poor tips.

Outside there is a commotion. One of the guards, at the head of the procession, is trying to dismount, but has only got so far as sitting side-saddle and is holding on for dear life as his mount charges back up the road they have just come down. The other guards are making no effort to help their comrade; they are sitting tight upon their own restless steeds, waiting, impatiently, either to rest or be off again, depending on their orders. Now, in the distance, you can see the guard has finally dismounted and the horse is charging toward the inn, again, with him in tow caught up amongst the reins and other straps, bouncing, twisting and somersaulting on the muddy road, sending up a spray like a water skier. The other guards, and their horses, watch nonchalantly, not daring to move until they are told to. The King is unperturbed and continues to sip at his coffee without a word. Up the path, to the head of the procession once more and the horse halts and then allows the guard to untangle himself from the reins. The guard, whose uniform was once blue like the others, stands up, adjusts his clothing as though to smarten himself and then walks away from the horse without shouting or glaring at anyone. The others remain seated, stiff to attention, averting their eyes from their bedraggled companion. Out of sight, for a second, then reappearing in the doorway, the unicoloured guard steps into the inn like a mythical swamp monster, trailing brown mush behind him. He salutes the King, spraying wet dirt into your face, and bellows out, 'Your carriage is ready for you, my liege.'

'You are not wearing your helmet, guard,' the King snaps at him.

'No, my liege. It fell from my head and lies a way up the road. I thought it best to report to you before I go fetch it, my liege,' the guard replies timorously.

'This is a shabby show. I saw you had trouble with your horse.'

'Yes, my liege. It was a little joke. My mount sought to humiliate me as a rebuke.'

'Well he most certainly succeeded. You looked a damn fool splashing about in the mud like that and now you look like a large pile of dung standing before me. I will not demote you for it, you will retain your command, however, I insist that you ride with the rear guard and select someone else to lead for the time being. And, I suggest that you improve your relationship with your horse. We cannot have him teaching you how to run things now, can we? Teaching you a little respect, eh!' The King is stern, but there is a tinge of humour in his tone. 'Go fetch your helmet and rearrange your troop. By the time you are done, we will be out and ready to leave. Dismissed.'

'Yes, my liege.' The guard turns and marches out, trying to keep what dignity he has left.

'Our horses can be terribly temperamental at times,' King Berthold IX says to you, 'and their passion for a good joke can become a trifle tedious. They like to laugh, but we humans find their sense of humour a little difficult to understand.' He is wearing a quizzical expression and is genuinely puzzled. 'Can you see what I mean. Look at them chucking to themselves. They find it so bloody funny to disgrace the troops. It amazes me how we manage to maintain a cavalry at all. They're so rebellious, ill-disciplined, no sense of order, they just do as they please.'

You can see an element of mirth in the relaxed manner of the horses, especially in contrast to their joyless, apprehensive riders. They stand loosely in formation like a group of students waiting for a class to start. Beyond them, the mud-covered guard is running further and further up the road.

'It is just as well our army is just for show, we deplore wars but need to display our willingness to fight to protect our sovereignty. I would prefer not to have a comedy show army, though.' He stares out of the window for a short time, shaking his head in disappointment at what he is seeing. 'Barkeeper,' hollers the King unexpectedly. 'Barkeeper. Ah, there you are. See to it our dunnage is loaded onto the carriage. We leave as soon as it is done,' he turns back to you and continues, 'Oh, what I would give for a quiet horse. My kingdom I suppose. A quiet horse that doesn't demand respect every time you bloody try to ride it. One that doesn't make you say please every time you want to turn left or right or else it heads for low branches at a gallop.' He drains his golden mug and then shouts, 'Service. Bring me more coffee. More bloody coffee I say.' Almost instantly, another silver tray with another golden mug upon it is brought over. The King makes the swap and goes on drinking, not stopping to swallow until the second mug is also empty. 'Right,' he says, 'Let's be off. We have a hard day's travel ahead.'

The carriage is warm and luxurious. Red velvet, deeply padded seats spread across the full width of the carriage from door to door. Above the doors are small oak wood cabinets with diamond-studded knobs and intricate carvings of the monarchy's coat of arms. Large, puffy cushions, of the same red velvet, serve as arm rests or pillows if the need arises and bear the same coat of arms neatly embroidered in gold and silver thread. The floor is covered by a tapestry-like carpet; a great battle being depicted in all its bloodthirsty glory.

The King has entered before you and has sprawled out on the seat to the right, so that he will be facing forward when the procession moves off. You have the seat to the left to yourself. The door is shut behind you by a steward who remains standing on the step of the carriage, as he will for the entire journey. His counterpart mimics his gargoyle pose on the other side, also watching the door to make sure it does not fly open while you are going along. The King leans out of the window, having noticed that you are comfortably seated, and shouts to the front of the line, 'To the palace and hurry.'

The realm of King Berthold IX could be considered a pretty place, with rolling hills, rivers and lakes and high mountains in the far, far distance signifying the border. It is green and lush with thousands of varieties of vegetation, displaying good evidence of plenty of rainfall. The rain is hammering down now, drumming hard on the roof of the carriage and obscuring vision beyond a few yards outside the window. Dark, grey clouds have sunk very low, threatening to settle on the ground as a thick, impenetrable fog. The wind is not too strong, but enough to rock the carriage from side to side, bringing the nauseous effect of a boat on a turbulent sea. The weather is as miserable as the guards who have to stay out in it.

The King is keeping you occupied with conversation about his country. About the tourist trade, which is expanding so rapidly that he has had to put a curb on building developments. About the farmers who are exporting the native crops all over the world now and about his loyal and efficient staff who have helped him maintain his country's wealth and happiness since his father died, over forty years ago. He also goes into how his people have resisted technology, fearing that it will destroy their way of life, their culture, beliefs, talents and eventually ecology, and the King is clearly in complete agreement with them. Some of the creatures and plant life, unique to these lands, are described to you and where you are likely to witness them first hand. Creatures as magnificent as dragons and plant life that is as insignificant as a weird blue mould, that alchemists use to colour their concoctions. He then starts to talk about the school of mystic arts, saying how that is where the limit of his knowledge and understanding lies.

'I could never get my head round the strange ordering of the bloody words, nor could I get my tongue to twist round the bloody peculiar pronunciation of them. All the extra phonemes you have to learn, the clicking noises at the back of your throat and such. Mysterious breed, these magicians. Too bloody mysterious. They never talk, except to summon demons or change mud into wine. And they always have to disappear. Just vanish, never telling you if and when they're ever coming back. Unreliable, unreliable they are. Not that I'm saying they're untrustworthy. Oh no, I believe they're honourable people, kind and decent the most part, only the occasional necromancer or witch and they tend to be just as reclusive and difficult to find, too. They never seem to trouble anyone, except to scare the shit out of the odd farmer or cocky adventurer. Care for another drink, Captain? Allow me to refill your glass. Good stuff, eh? Keeps you warm. What was I saying, ah yes, I have a court-magician. My wife, Queen Isabella. She is extraordinarily beautiful. Youthful looking and aged as I. Long, silver hair reaches to her ankles and her complexion is that of a new born baby. Her apprentice, Somermon, no Sewerman, oh whatever his name is, he will be going along with you on this mission. He's a young man, seems a bit dopey to me, but I think you'll like him.'

The carriage suddenly comes to a dead halt and the inertia almost throws the King into your lap. He curses vehemently and thrusts his head out one of the windows, demanding an explanation with a terrifying shout. The filthy, wet guard walks up from the rear and conveys the situation.

'It's the horses, my liege. They have decided they need a rest and will go no further until they are ready. I tried to persuade them to continue, but they just threatened to unseat me and then trample me to death,' explains the guard in a forlorn and desperate voice.

'Very well, guard,' replies the King, 'They may have ten minutes, no more.' He then hurries out of the carriage to use a convenient bush at the roadside.

You look the other way, out of the other windows, at a lacerated sky. In the distance a storm is raging.

'Don't worry, Captain. It won't reach us,' the King says as he is climbing back in, 'The aliens are testing their bloody weather control device. This rain won't slow us down, too much. We'll be at the palace before you know it.'

It is the gleaming rows of trumpets and horns that first catch your eye, then suddenly they sound a fanfare that ripples crisply to your ears. Scouts have taken news to the palace of the King's arrival and the greeting has begun, even though you are nearly a mile away. The royal musicians stand shoulder to shoulder either side of the road like overdressed bushes in their blue, white and gold tunics and matching floppy hats. They define the winding path the procession must take for the entire distance from where you are now, to where you will be. Despite the wind and rain they blow, standing rigid as posts for the flags that flap about on each of their instruments. Out in the muddy farmland and through the sodden streets of the town around the palace, through the enormous golden gates and spectacular grounds, into the courtyard the lines of musicians lead, each one blaring out a tuneful welcome.

King Berthold IX, now in his official role, waves regally to the crowds from behind a carriage window and smiles warmly at them until they are out of sight and the golden gates have shut.

'Welcome to my home, I trust you will find it comfortable,' the King says to you as the door, facing the palace, is opened by the steward.

The musicians have been left behind and are replaced by frilly-dressed servants. They stand either side of the red carpet leading up the polished marble steps into the palace reception hall. Above the steps is a canopy of polished marble, held up upon columns of carved, polished marble, creating a space that the rain cannot reach. The Queen, court advisers and knights wait at the top of the great steps, dignified and solemn with formality.

The King jumps from the carriage and leaps up the first few steps to the palace. He then stops, turns and looks at you. 'Come on, come on,' he says, 'We've got a feast to eat before we send you off to dish it out to the aliens.'

Sir Prancealot is losing his patience. He has come over and is trying to help you onto your horse, but the creature is stubborn and moves away each time you swing yourself up to seat yourself on her back. For the fourth time you descend toward the stable floor, fortunately with Sir Prancealot there to break your fall. In a tangle of limbs and hard metal armour you both struggle to pick yourselves up off the filthy, straw covered ground. Your intended mount finds this incredibly amusing, neighing openly at you, throwing her head back in mirth, swishing her tail excitedly and stamping her left fore-hoof in the dirt in way of applause. All the other horses share in your horse's hilarity, making the stable seem, oddly, like an auditorium with a class comedy act performing. Sir Prancealot is not seeing the humour in the scenario, however. He hastily helps you to stand and makes a humble apology to you while he dusts you off. He then walks to meet your horse face to face and appeals to her to behave.

'Come now, Mici,' he says in an endearing tone. 'You understand the importance of this mission and you know that it is an urgent one. The whole of the kingdom and the planet is threatened and we have not got time for fun and games. Please, try to behave yourself for the next few days, we can have all the fun in the world once we have defeated our enemy.'

'Oh, fine,' replies the horse, indignantly, after the last few tittering neighs, 'but, don't blame me if the foreigner can't stay on. I can't compensate for the lack of skill of the rider.'

Sir Prancealot beckons you with a wave of his hand and then successful aids you to climb upon your mount, which has knelt down to make the task easier. When she stands you feel a slight sensation of vertigo that wears off just as quickly.

'Hi. Call me Mici,' she says heartily, twisting her head around to fix one eye on you, 'It's short for Micalwish Nutear. I'll go as easy as I can on you, just don't kick me, squeeze me or pull on my mane, that clear?' You nod in agreement and Mici moves off to follow the others into the courtyard.

Outside, the brightness of the blazing sun dazzles you, though there is very little warmth in its rays. Already, you are feeling uncomfortable and keep slipping sideways from the saddle. Mici jostles about beneath you trying to help you balance. As your eyes become accustomed to the sunlight, in the courtyard and beyond the golden gates you notice crowds of people waiting to give your party a good send-off; a complete contrast to the dingy, partitioned, claustrophobic conditions of the stable. There are thousands of people clapping and cheering you and your group as you embark upon the first leg of your journey. Sir Prancealot leads the eight knights, the magician and yourself before the King and Queen, who stand high up on the balcony of the palace, overlooking the courtyard. He salutes, they wave and then you are trotting away through the golden gates and the encouraging throng. It is not until you have travelled over two hilltops, not until the palace and the buildings all around it are far out of sight that the sounds of the multitudes fade from the air.

You ride in pairs now the road is clear. Sir Curidge rides beside you, mounted on Sevourn Nostidiposi: a lean, swift, perpetually suspicious horse which keeps a distance from you for fear of bumping into you. Sir Curidge shouts friendly comments to you, but you miss most of what he says because of the continually changing gap between you, the sound of the thundering hoof steps and the noise of the wind in your ears. Directly ahead of you is Sir Angost riding upon Dunsed Strom and to his left is Sir Shipton on Runbettul Trewa. Ahead of them is Sir Prancealot upon Rhad Sa Lanis, who leads the field; riding beside them are Sir Jovien and Yalwas Phypa, who despite the pace are singing lively songs of battle and victory into the wind.

Around you the landscape is changing. The rolling, grassy

hills are turning rocky and barren; the mud of the road is hard and holds no water at all. The trees are thinning out; the types altering into gnarled, leafless varieties. The climbs are steeper and steeper and the terrain rises, steadily, in altitude. The hills are higher and the valleys deeper; the possibility of a fall is made more precarious. The road meanders around the base of hillsides and to the peaks of valleys, heading in the general direction of the not so distant mountains.

The sun is sinking to the horizon on your left; the reflection of the pink, white, blue sky shimmers on the silvery surface of an expansive lake. Conifer trees predominate the southern bank and sweep around to enclose the far, eastern end. A mountainside rises up from the northern bank, too steep and rocky for much plant life to take hold. The nearest bank has a few trees and a pebble shore.

Sir Prancealot calls for a halt. Pseudomin, the magician, has fallen far, far behind; his horse, Zaly Stabard, is rather reluctant to keep with the pace. Sir Veneric and his horse have stayed with them; Sipsang Dwin, chatting away, heartily, with the magician's mount.

'The light will be failing, soon,' Sir Prancealot proclaims to the waiting group. 'We will set a camp near the shoreline, amongst those trees. Jovien and Trepid cook tonight. Curidge, Hardgrip and Angost go hunting. Shipton, the Captain and I will build shelter. Veneric and Pseudomin can do the washing-up. While the humans make camp the horses may wander down to the waterfront to drink and graze upon the available vegetation.'

With the commands having been given, everyone sets about their assigned tasks, briskly. Rhad Sa Lanis expertly finds the easiest route through the rocks and between the trees, pauses to allow Sir Prancealot to dismount and then goes on into the lake and stands knee deep, stooping his head to drink. The other, now riderless, horses follow suit; Phaevercity dashes ahead to splash about in the lake, the rest spread out along the shoreline like heroic equine monuments. Mici goes further, forgetting you are still seated upon her back. The water rises to her belly, above your ankles, she walks on, not stopping to drink or to let you off.

'Going for a swim, Mici?' calls Freddaul Easte, Sir Trepid's mount, with a bestial smirk. It is a peculiar sound, the sound of horses giggling to themselves.

Mici halts, turns and faces the others and you could swear she is grinning, mischievously. 'Yes,' she replies, 'I think it will be quite refreshing after that long run.'

She continues on, the lake rising up to her neck and above your waist. It is cold, very cold and very, very refreshing. You can hear the laughter echoing from the mountainside and from the source on the shore. Deepthroated laughter, cut by occasional neighs. It is a strange noise that is becoming far too familiar. Mici thrusts herself into deeper water and you slip, ungracefully, backwards, and to the side a little, with an explosive splash and pitiful yelp. The waves of laughter surge over you as you break above the surface gasping, desperately, for air.

Drenched and humiliated you traipse back to shore, listening to the roars of mirth in appreciation for the entertainment that you have just provided. Sir Prancealot is standing, hands on hips, on the pebble beach waiting with obvious impatience for you to reach him.

'Come along, Captain,' he barks, 'We need help building the shelter. Bring some of that wood over to the camp site and hurry. We have less than an hour of daylight left.'

A few moments of aggravation aside, the branch roof shelters are constructed with organised ease. Sir Prancealot and Sir Shipton step back to admire the result; hands on hips they sigh, simultaneously, with satisfaction.

'A good job done, eh, Sir Shipton?'

'I am pleased to agree, Sir Prancealot, and I have worked up a healthy appetite. I'm famished.'

'Well, let's hope Sirs Jovien and Trepid have done as good a job with dinner as we have with these shelters. What do you think, Captain?'

These shelters are not palaces, nor even suitable stables. The neatly bound branches will guide water into the sheltered areas rather than out and a strong-ish gust of wind would, easily, tare the roofs off and the walls would not stand up without them. Inside, the beds are very itchy looking blankets with leaves beneath acting as a mattress. A night in this structure could prove restless and tormenting amongst the bugs, mice and spiders. With diplomacy, you try to tell them what you think. Sir Prancealot and Sir Shipton look at each other, smugly.

'Don't worry, Captain,' Sir Prancealot assures you, 'we'll get Pseudomin to cast a spell on it before we retire. He'll turn it into a lovely row of cottages, but he needs the basic frames to work on.'

The enormous camp fire beats back the darkness and provides some warmth to the night air around it. You pull your saddle closer to the flames and sit upon it, allowing the heat to dry off your clothes. The clearing is reasonably enclosed, only a gentle breeze blows about you and the clouds, for the time being, are withholding their rain. Above the campfire is the most gigantic shish kebab you have ever seen; whole rabbits, chickens, lizards and fish are skewered by a metal spear, being turned occasionally by Sir Trepid. In the fire are giant potatoes, roasting nicely, and two large pots, containing the boiling vegetables. Sir Trepid is flustered. He stirs, prods and turns like an overcautious whirlwind, talking to himself in nervous anxiety about getting everything cooked right.

Sir Jovien is cracking open bottles of wine, singing songs of courage and endeavour as he passes the mugs around. He is, obviously, making them up as he goes along and he improvises a verse for you as he fills your mug and hands it to you,

'Take this mug of wine, my friend,
'Cause tomorrow could see your end,
Drink 'till you're drunk and enjoy this night,
'Cause by tomorrow you'll be in a fight.
Hoorah, hoorah, hoorah, hoorah,
Tomorrow we go to kick some arse.'

The last two lines become a chorus and all the other knights join in singing,

'Hoorah, hoorah, hoorah, hoorah,
Tomorrow we go to kick some arse.'

After the fifth repetition, Sir Jovien holds a tremendous high note for the last hoorah while the other knights sing the last line and they finish together in perfect cadence.

'Long live King Berthold the Ninth,' bellows Sir Curidge, 'and Queen Isabella, protectors of this realm.'

'Long live the King and Queen!' shout the others in unison, before they all tip their mugs and gulp down the contents.

Out of the darkness between the trees, Sir Veneric and Pseudomin finally arrive.

'Well, it's good to see you both,' calls out Sir Jovien to them. 'We thought we might have lost you.'

'You very nearly did,' answers Sir Veneric, 'I am thankful you were singing or else we would never have found you.'

'So, what kept you?' Sir Shipton asks, after they have dismounted.

'A couple of reasons,' replies Sir Veneric, 'mainly it was Pseudomin's horse ...'

'Yes. He wasn't named Zaly Stabard for nothing,' cuts in Pseudomin, resentfully.

'... and we were also held up by another horse,' continues Sir Veneric. 'Quite a terrifying looking animal. Said its name was Tremighan and it was asking after the Captain, here,' he points at you, 'then it got dark, of course.'

'Well, have a drink and a sing-song with us,' says Sir Jovien as he passes two full mugs to them, 'and come sit by the fire. Dinner is almost ready.' He starts to sing a new song of bravery and honour and then goes over to help Sir Trepid dish out the meals.

Pseudomin sits, on the ground, between you and Sir Shipton and rubs his tired legs through his robe. Sir Veneric goes to retrieve their saddles and baggage from the horses.

'So, you had trouble with your horse, eh, Pseudomin?' Sir Shipton asks him in a mocking tone.

'Yes, he was determined to go slower every hour and stop to graze more and more often. I threaten to turn him into a weasel, but he just said, "Good, then you can carry me." The cheek of it. I should have done something to him, but I couldn't think of anything appropriate.'

'Ha, ha, ha. Yes, horses can be a bit facetious at times. Runbettul Trewa, my horse, is just as bad, though in different ways. He does like to have his moments of activity, testing my riding skills to the limit. He'll suddenly start bucking and rearing, jumping about, stop-starting, almost anything to make the ride "more exciting" as he puts it. Too often I have fallen and been the butt of his joke. At least Sir Veneric stayed with you, eh.'

'Hmm. I don't know whether that was a good thing. I appreciated his company, but his horse is a little too vocal from both ends.'

'Yes. Sipsang Dwin does like to talk a lot,' comments Sir Shipton amidst his own laughter.

A plate, piled high with perfectly cooked food, reaches you and the conversation is intermingled with the sound of smacking lips, loud swallowing, full mouths and belching. The wine flows continuously and the songs involve more vulgarity as the night goes on. The horses are at the edge of the firelight, having a noisy party of their own. Sir Shipton returns to the conversation about the horses after a few mouthfuls of lizard.

'It's Sir Trepid I feel most for. His mount, Freddaul Easte, has helped get him that complex he has developed,' he calls over to Sir Trepid. 'Come and join us, Sir Trepid. Come and tell us about your horse.'

Warily, Sir Trepid steps over to your small group and sits, carefully, in the gap you have created for him. 'W- w- what do, do you want to know?' he asks, timidly.

'Tell us about what happened on your way back from Maykor,' Sir Shipton requests and then he turns to you and explains, 'It's a straight journey, one road which connects the palace with this town, only a few miles, nothing perilous about it.'

Sir Trepid seems uncomfortable with all the attention focused on him. Sir Veneric and Sir Curidge are also nearby and have been listening intently. Sir Jovien and Sir Prancealot are on the other side of the camp fire making a song and dance about the journey so far not paying any notice, but the other knights have turned their concentration to what Sir Trepid is about to say.

'Well, er ... I, I was coming home ... to, to the palace,' he starts, meekly, 'taking the, the main road ...'

'Speak up!' shouts Sir Curidge. 'Sir Veneric can hardly hear you.'

Slightly louder, Sir Trepid continues, 'yes, er ... YES. Well, I got to, to the crossroads, near, near Dungton ... It was about, er ... er ... midday and, and Fred wanted to, to rest. He, he grazed while I boiled some w-water for some, some tea to go with my sand- sandwiches, which I had bought back at a, a roadside stable. Well, er ... well, Fred started on about going the wrong, wrong way, that we had, had taken a wrong turn and, and we were heading aw- away from the palace. I, I told him to l- l- look at the, the signpost, but he, he insisted that some filthy robber had turned the sign round, he, he could see where, where the ground was disturbed. He then went on about, how, how the direction we were head- heading smelled funny and, and that there were, prob- probably, fifty bandits waiting to ambush us, fur- further up the road.'

'Didn't like the odds, eh, Sir Trepid?' cuts in Sir Angost with a venomous smirk.

'Well ... well, I didn't want to bel- believe him, but, but ...'

'But, he convinced you to take an alternative route. A longer, harder, more dangerous one,' finishes Sir Angost for him.

'Er ...yes. Yes, through Draken Valley.'

The knights, who are listening, burst into loud laughter at this and jibe Sir Trepid about going red with embarrassment.

'I'd rather fight off fifty robbers,' shouts out Sir Curidge.

'I'd rather ride behind Sir Veneric for a week,' calls out Sir Hardgrip, bringing a fresh upsurge of laughter from the knights.

After a while, their merriment subsides and Sir Shipton wipes his eyes and says, 'Sir Trepid, Sir Trepid, please continue. What happened when you got there?'

'Well, er ...' he answers, 'er, we were just entering the valley when he, Fred, started saying that something was watching us and he was getting scared. We, we went on a mile, or so, but he, he was acting really jittery and I was t-terrified. He kept saying he smelled evil dragons, hungry ones with fiery breath. I had had enough and was ordering him to take me back to the c-crossroads and he, he finally agreed when we could both hear the fl-fla-flapping of dragon's wings. Fred ran like a d-demented r-rabbit and I gripped m-my arms around his n-n-neck, h-holding on for d-dear life. He got us t-to the t-tree line and we were only a l-little s-s-singed.'

'You grown your hair back, yet?' heckles Sir Angost.

'Er ... er, yes. Most of it,' replies Sir Trepid.

'So, then what happened?' asks Sir Shipton.

'Well, er ... well, we came back t-to the m-main road, where Fred started on about the f-fifty rob-robbers ag-again. I-I was still sh-shaken by the dragon, th-thinking that it might have f-f-followed us and it was g-getting d-dark. I s-set up-c-camp, without a f-f-fire and s-stood watch all n-n-night, while F-F-Fred went t-to s-sleep.' Sir Trepid pauses while some of the knights snigger. He goes on, 'Well, er.. morning c-came and I-I was t-tired and aching. F-Fred was well rested, s-s-sprightly and ready t-t-to t-take on an army. Every time I s-started t-to n-n-nod off he, he would wake me, sh-shouting that we were under attack. "B-bandits," he'd sh-shout, "b-bandits, wake up." T-Twenty sh-shocks later I wised up t-to his prank and went back t-to s-s-sleep each t-time after. But, then he, he woke me one t-time and we were g-galloping of the road. "They're b-behind us he," he yelled, "hold t-tight." He, he ran down, down a, a s-steep hillside, over a s-stream, through a f-field of f-f-full g-grown maize and headed as f-fast as he, he could g-go at a hedge reaching above the height of my head. I-I p-pleaded with him t-to s-s-stop, b-but he insisted he, he c-could jump it, s-so on he went. He, he was about t-to l-l-leap when he s-said, said, "Maybe you're right," and s-s-suddenly s-stops, th-throwing me d-directly into the hedge.'

The knights have erupted, again, tears of laughter roll down their cheeks as they clunk about the floor in their heavy armour. Sir Trepid looks, shyly, down into the mug of wine he holds in his hands.

'How long did it take for you to crawl out?' Sir Angost teases in a sarcastic tone.

'Er ... er ... ab-about th-th-three, maybe f-f-four hours,' Sir Trepid replies, without lifting his head. The cacophony of jeering knights rises in volume.

'And, what type of bush was it?' taunts Angost, again.

'A, a haw-hawthorn, I-I think'

'And, were the bandits following you?'

'N-no.'

It is very late by the time the knights settle down to occasional outbursts and witty comments. The remainder of the story is delivered by the other knights, in staggered segments, in between bouts of spontaneous giggling. Sir Trepid had returned to the palace trembling, bruised and lacerated. He had lost his helmet, gauntlets, sword and codpiece in the hedge and it had taken several weeks for him to recover from his injuries. On his first journey out, in escort of the collected taxes, the dragon showed up, blasted him with fire, took the gold and flew off. You also ascertain that this incident took place a long time ago and many more incidents have happened since then.

The roasting flames of the fire reduce to glowing cinders and the party agrees it is time to retire. Sir Prancealot requests Pseudomin to perform an incantation, including many intricate movements, confusing gestures and incomprehensible pronunciations, so to turn the fragile tree branch and twine constructions into a neat row of cottages. With dramatic emphasis, Pseudomin bellows out the last words and stops waving his arms about. The wooden structures spontaneously and simultaneously combust. The flames lick around each branch in every shelter, the twine turns to puffs of smoke and like a house of cards, in a light breeze they collapse. Upon the pyres, you can see tiny, people-shaped flames, dancing in a circle. They are singing at such a high pitch you can hardly hear it. The knights gaze on, mutely, not even twitching in an effort to dampen the flames.

'This isn't quite what I had in mind,' sighs Sir Prancealot, breaking the tension after a long period of staring. The hilarity that the horses are experiencing has just become very clear and loud. 'This isn't at all what I had in mind, in fact. Where do you propose we sleep now, Pseudomin?'

'I'm terribly sorry everyone,' Pseudomin whimpers. 'The words for fire-sprite and the words for cottage are very similar in the magical language. I must have mispronounced. If you all gather some piles of leaves together, I'll try and make them beds.' His pleas for trust go unheeded by the knights who are, politely, declining his offer. They use their saddles as pillows and sleep in their armour and within a few minutes they are all unconscious, snoring deeply. Pseudomin is muttering to himself, trying to remember how to exorcise sprites. You alone heard the steps of an approaching animal. It is behind you and very close.

In a grave, deep, echoing tone that you would expect from the living dead, the words, 'I've found you. Outside, alone and at night. You're mine, now,' drift over your shoulder, carrying with them the scent of burning meat.

Your reflection is slightly distorted by the convex surface of the large oval mirror. The light is bright behind you, making a silhouette of your image; it is a moment before you recognise your own features. With more scrutiny, you are able to discern the curved, yellow lines as window frames and that it is daylight that floods in through them. You turn, slowly, to your left, studying the familiar environment around you. The yellow cupboards and white work surface with plates and utensils organised, neatly, into racks, upon it. Turning fully around, you see the windows with the chromium sink and draining board below them; the back door to the side. In the wall to your left is another door. The door is closed, but you can hear the chimes of a clock, in the next room, drifting back into silence again once they cease. It is so quiet you can hear the clock ticking.

You look out of the window; over the fence, to the soft, blue sky, at the puffy, white trail of an aeroplane. It is very far away and high up and you can hear the drone of its engines despite the windows being shut. Upon the window ledge is a washing-up liquid bottle and cleaning utensils; a dry, sick flower stands limply in a crystal vase beside them. On the sideboard, upturned, lie a yellow cup and saucer. On the work surface, in the corner, stands a white kettle with its gauge indicating empty.

Time seems to have stopped. The clock continues ticking, the aeroplane continues to rumble through the air and very, very slowly, the flower is crumbling to dust. If not stopped, then slowed down. Diminished to an eerie pace.

A gate creaks open, slams shut and you can hear someone ascending the wooden stairs, on the other side of the back door. Fourteen steps and staring through the glass panel, in the upper half of the door, is a woman. She is gaunt, shabby; her hair has not been washed, or combed, in what appears to be months, or even years. She opens the door and steps in, locking it behind her. Her long dress is light blue, but filthy, and she wears a yellow-brown cardigan with bright, red sleeves from wrist to elbow. In her right hand, she has a large kitchen knife, red with wet, fresh blood. Both her hands, the front of her dress, her shoes, all soaked in blood. She does not seem to notice you. Water gushes from the tap and you see her take the washing-up liquid from the window sill and begin to wash the knife. The bottle falls from her grasp into the sink and she whirls round with the knife clasped in both hands, pointing it, threateningly, at you.

'You,' she says, in a prolonged hiss. 'You. What are you doing here? I hate you, you shit. It's your fault, you did it. I hate you, hate you, you shit-bag.' Her tone of loathing is chilling, like ice melting down your neck. 'I'll teach you. I'll teach you,' she promises as she edges over to the door, removes the key and tucks it in her cardigan pocket. 'You need to learn, yes, you shit, you need to learn some things. I saw you. I saw you do it. You need to be punished for it. Punished, so you don't forget.'

The blade catches the sunlight as she suddenly lunges at you, making you react before you would have. The blade slices over your forearm, a thrust intended for your abdomen. She is a wild shadow, screaming like a banshee; the running water drums against the plastic bottle and the clock, in the other room, chimes again. You have sustained several deep cuts in your attempts to wrestle the blade from your attacker, and she has taken to biting and scratching to gain the advantage. She is savage, clawing at your eyes and throat, snarling and spitting, screaming and shouting how she will teach you, punish you for what you have done.

The knife is in your hand. The woman has got you off balance and is trying to gnaw your ear. You both fall. Her piercing scream is gripped with pain and denial. She stares at the handle protruding from her stomach as she rolls, onto her back, away from you. The pool of blood around her grows, she clasps the handle and eases the blade from within her, grunting and hissing and finally a terrifying scream of relief when the knife is free.

'Wake up, Captain. Wake up.' Sir Curidge has begun to shake you; relatively gently for a knight who has had his sleep disturbed. 'You were dreaming. Something terrible, judging by the noise you were making. It'll be daylight, soon, it's not really worth going back to sleep. We might as well get a fire started, so we can breakfast early. We'll try to entice one or two of those fire sprites to help us.'

Without his helmet, Sir Curidge's face seems soft and handsome in the half-moon light. His thick, long black hair drapes around his shoulders, bringing more definition to his square jaw line and perfectly shaped nose. He is the only one up. You try to apologise for disturbing him, but he just replies, 'Not at all, not at all. I am grateful. It's better to be awoken by your involuntary screams than by Sir Jovien's singing. Come on, let's get some wood.'

Only the moon and stars spare you from fumbling about a thicket in total darkness. Further down, towards the shore, you can see the little, dancing lights of the fire sprites and hear their chirpy voices carrying through the crisp, clean mountain air. All the wood is damp; the fine mist from the lake has saturated in through the bark, leaving it slimy to the touch and completely un-ignitable. Sir Curidge dismisses the difficulty with a casual laugh and a comment on how the fire sprites wouldn't care if it were wet, dry or frozen. Grazing like cows through a field, you collect the dead branches and deliver them to the camp fire site, which is only a pile of smouldering ashes, now. Sir Curidge begins to collect more small boulders to surround the growing mound of firewood and you continue collecting wood for a stockpile, to be used when what is there is all consumed.

'A task well done, I would say,' self-commends Sir Curidge as he stands beside you, admiring the conical construction of dead, twisted tree limbs. 'I am truly gratefully for your assistance and I am joyous having been in such wonderful company. There have been very few who have enticed me the way you do.' His eyes convince you that his words are genuine. 'You are strong, powerful, graceful and glorious. You are more beautiful than any other person I have had the pleasure of meeting. The sound of your voice enchants me, the gaze from your eyes beguiles me and my heart pounds like the drums of Cahlcahla when your very presence is near mine.' He reaches out and clasps your hands, gently, in his. You come closer together, he lifts your hands to his lips and kisses them. Passionate arms wrap around your waist and you accept his embrace. Dexterously, you undo all the bindings and each piece of his suit of armour falls away.

Now nude, you both run down to the lake and jump in and swim to a more secluded part of the shoreline. Dawn is over an hour away. Wet, shivering, you both climb up onto the dry, soft sand of a small beach, hidden by a huge willow tree in full life. You cling to each other for warmth and then kiss. Lowering yourselves to the ground, without breaking contact, you continue caressing each other into a state of loving excitement.

The sky is brightening and you are swimming back to the camp; sustaining the occasional pecking attacks of the local ducks attempting to 'shoo' you away from their territory. There is barely a ripple on the surface of the lake, only the wake of your passage through the water. The others are still asleep, you can hear them all snoring as you approach the shore. Dripping with freezing water, again, you follow Sir Curidge to the stockpile of wood, take two branches and then go over to the ashes of the would-be cottages where the fire sprites are at play.

'Now, this is where our plans develop a level of difficulty. These fiery demons are notoriously mischievous and enjoy the art of deception. And- and unless, you can speak their tongue, we will not be able to persuade them to ignite our branches, gently,' Sir Curidge explains to you.

The sprites have noticed your approach and are gathering at the edge of the cinders, nearest you. Sir Curidge, stealthily, moves in, the branch extended at full arms stretch. 'Be careful when you prod,' he instructs over his shoulder, 'I have no doubt that some of these flaming devils will try to jump upon your skin. Once they have no fuel to consume, or have been extinguished with water, they will be banished back to the ethereal world. They may also try running up the stick instead of igniting it, so be ready to drop the stick if they do. Watch closely, now.'

Sir Curidge lunges forward and pokes the crowd of brightly glowing, extremely excitable, fiery little people. Two have attempted a run up the branch, but Sir Curidge reacts, quickly, and a third tries a heroic leap, landing like a lemming on the stony ground. In a flash it is gone, returned to the plane from which it came. You glance back at Sir Curidge and see he has the situation well in hand. In one, swift stroke of the branch, in his left hand, he has lifted one of the sprites from the other branch and, now, they are passively burning like torches, held high in triumph. 'Easy as that,' he gloats. 'Your turn, Captain.'

The fire sprites anticipate your actions. As you lunge forward with a branch, you see a swarm of flames spring towards you. Your weight is forward and you cannot pull back. They all land, with absolute precision, in an impressive inverse pyramid, balancing upon one sprites shoulders, who is delicately balanced on the end of your twisted, wooden foil. With hesitant steps, they advance up the stick.

'Drop the stick and run like your arse is on fire!' shouts Sir Curidge at you.

You judge his advice as sound and do exactly that.

Finally, the fire is alight, the two sprites, obtained by Sir Curidge, are happy in their new combustible home. The sun has risen above the horizon and the other knights are jumping up ready for breakfast, brought into wakefulness by the cheery sound of Sir Jovien's voice, singing an up-tempo song about early birds, worms and the best time for battle. As one naked mob they charge into the lake. Bathed and refreshed they charge back, again, to climb, shivering like lambs, into their undergarments. Sitting in a steaming circle around the, now, blazing fire, they express their gratitude and strike up in song with Sir Jovien leaving Pseudomin and Sir Veneric to prepare the morning meal.

'The day for battle has just begun,

Won't be long before we're having fun.
Play your pipes, your fiddles, your flutes,
Then sharpen your swords and put on your suits.
Join us our brothers, join us our friends,
For then our joy will know no end,
And we'll all kick arse together,
Yes, we'll all kick arse together.'

Thick, lumpy porridge is the choice for breakfast. Huge bowls are passed round, and oversized wooden spoons to accompany them. Sir Hardgrip gives you a spoon from your left and Sir Curidge offers a bowl from your right. You take them in hand and contemplate eating the grey, bubbling mass put before you. As the knights begin to devour their portions, the noise of smacking lips, slurping and belching, helps your nausea grow and you push the bowl away from yourself.

'Do you have no appetite this morning?' asks Sir Curidge, to which you respond by shaking your head. 'Well I'm sure Hardgrip will appreciate it. Sir Hardgrip,' he calls over your shoulder, 'Sir Hardgrip. It appears there is a second helping available, would you care for it?'

'Oh, yes,' he answers. 'I'll have it if it's not wanted. I'm not scared of dragons, trolls, manticores, giant spiders, snakes or scorpions, nor of rocks falling from the sky or fire rushing from the ground, so I'll be damned if I'm scared of Pseudomin's cooking. Pass it here. Thank you. It doesn't taste so bad if you keep your eyes closed and don't breathe in while you put it in your mouth.' He resumes his eating with added zeal. You stare into the fire and try to block out the noise he is making. Fortunately, Sir Curidge has finished his breakfast and offers you conversation as a distraction.

'No. There is very little that fazes Hardgrip. He manages to ride that rather energetic mount, deal with seventeen children and three wives in two different towns and he is forever riding back and forth across the country nowadays. I remember the times before he was married and before he even had stables. We used to go off on quite a few adventures together. We once travelled to the furthest, southern limits of this realm, using the most difficult routes and facing danger every step of the way. However, it was not until we reached our journeys end, in the jungle, that we actually thought we might die together.' Sir Curidge leans back and contemplates the memories for a moment.

'Yes, we were set upon by a tribe of pygmies, who blew darts through pipes at us, with some sort of poison on them which sent us to sleep. I awoke tied to a spit, being basted in oil and sprinkled with seasoning. Hardgrip was no better off. He was trussed up like a turkey, watching a group of pygmies preparing an enormous amount of stuffing and preheating a gigantic stone oven. It was inconceivable that knights could beg for mercy, but that we did. They didn't understand a single word of what we said and began to cook us despite our ranting.' Sir Curidge pauses to drink some of the coffee that had been passed to him while he was talking. You accept a hot, clay mug from Sir Hardgrip and take a sip yourself. It is strong, very bitter and very hot.

'They released us, eventually,' Sir Curidge continues, 'but not before I had finished saying my prayers. They bathed us, provided a vegetarian feast and pampered us until we felt guilty about neglecting our duty to the King. They were the most friendly and welcoming people I have ever met. We call them the "Hibee Geebie" tribe, because of their uncommon way of welcoming a stranger to their home. They believe that once you have seen beyond your worst fears and suspicions of people, you become aware of all the good intentions and warm feelings from them, which is the basis of friendship. We were quite sad to leave as it happens.'

You and Sir Curidge discuss the philosophy of this tribe while the other knights clear everything away. They leave the camp fire for the fire sprites to devour, in way of showing their gratitude for the sprites' help in lighting it. Sir Prancealot then shouts for the horses. Rhad Sa Lanis comes at a run, followed by Dunsed Strom, Yalwas Phypa, Runbettul Trewa and Phaevercity. Sipsang Dwin, Freddaul Easte and Sevourn Nostidiposi approach at a trot and Zaly Stabard is just raising himself from the ground, slowly. Micalwish Nutear is nowhere to be seen. Freddaul Easte stops in front of you, before going over to Sir Trepid, to deliver a message.

'Mici has asked me to tell you that she has gone for a walk and that she will catch up with you. She said that this was such a beautiful place that she couldn't resist taking a look around. It seems you will have to walk for a while, Captain,' Fred says with, obvious, mockery in his tone.

There is that sound, again. The inhuman chuckling that enhances humiliation. Sir Prancealot steps into the scene, 'Come, now, calm down. Don't worry, Captain, we'll just have to wait while Fred goes to fetch her. Go on, Freddaul, we agreed to have fun after the mission.'

Freddaul Easte lifts his head high, snorts loudly, turns holding the pose and walks off, mumbling something about how miserable human beings are. You do not have to wait long, he is hardly beyond the tree line before he turns back with Micalwish Nutear beside him. She ambles up to you, stands rigid, waiting for you to climb into the saddle and then snaps, 'Come on then, get on. I've got better things to be doing than waiting around for you.'

Sir Prancealot helps you up and then implores your mount, again, 'Please, Mici, will you behave for the rest of the day.' He pats her on the neck and goes to climb upon the back of the statuesque Rhad Sa Lanis.

The group moves off, quickly, in single file, up the winding rocky path. It leads along the base of a cliff, to your right and along the top of one to your left. The path is narrowing, but your pace is sustained. You can see the drop is not that far, though the landing is upon rocks, with a thin stream trickling between them. The wind blows in heavy gusts, threatening to topple any one of you. With each sudden blast the pace slows. The cliff to your right is leaning over the path now, spooning the wind down on you all. Up ahead, the cliff seems to curl right over the path, forming a tunnel and protection from the wind. Strange, flickering crystals, set within the walls, provide a dim red illumination, instantaneously taking the place of daylight. You can barely see the horses up ahead, but you are nearly deafened by their echoing, clattering hoof steps.

On and on you weave through the mountainside, restricted to single file, feeling the dips and the rises of the ride in your belly. The passage grows tighter and you feel your clothing brush against the walls and see sparks fly from the armour of the knights up ahead.

Quite unexpectedly, the tunnel opens out into a huge, glistening cavern. The sound of galloping horses reverberates around the stalactites, stretching down from the unseeable ceiling, and the stalagmites that are rising out of the pools of still water on either side of the path. The echoes give the impression of a greater number of horses, approaching from a distance from an indeterminable direction. It is the stalactites that radiate a lime green spectral light within this underworld. Twisted limestone columns appear to hold the prickly ceiling from the spiny floor; you feel as though you are in the jaws of a living mountain. The air is warm and musty, carrying the scent of stagnation.

The cavern has only one other exit, leading into another tunnel no larger than the one you came in through. Sir Curidge glances off the wall as he enters the narrow passage, Sevourn Nostidiposi comes to an abrupt halt ahead of you, so as not to bring harm to his rider or himself, and you are almost catapulted onto them by Mici's attempt to avoid collision. Stunned, you slip from her back onto the hard cavern floor. Only Sir Prancealot and Sir Angost preceded Sir Curidge and all the remaining knights have stopped in their tracks, dismounted and have come over to check that you are not injured. Still dazed, you realise that they are pulling you out of the water and are helping you to remount your horse.

Then you are off again, the harsh clap of horse-shoe hitting stone returns to a deafening volume and you race on as though you are being chased by a horde of goblins, pounding through the dim, tight tunnel, clinging to life by grasping around Mici's neck. Sir Hardgrip is now ahead of you and you cannot see anyone ahead of him. Coming out of a sharp bend, you are dazzled by daylight and then, suddenly, burst from the claustrophobic conditions of the tunnels into the agoraphobic atmosphere of a snow-laden mountaintop, looking out over the land as far as the eye can see.

You are near the summit of one of the highest mountains in the range. The sky is clear and you are able to see over the top of others to other lands and the sea, which is many miles away to the southwest. Below, is a deep, wide valley with a white-water river running through its centre. On the other side, exposed, is the source of your mission. The alien base. A massive complex of inter-connected, grey metal buildings. In the middle sits a huge, white dome, nearly a sphere, sparkling in the midday sunlight. A causeway leads from the compound to a landing site where two alien spacecraft are sitting dormant. Another tubular structure extends to a building in the river. You presume they are harnessing it's natural power to supply their base. You ride on, down to the tree line, where at a convenient clearing Sir Prancealot calls everyone to a halt. The party needs to rest and plan their infiltration.

'Great ride, eh, Sir Trepid,' says Sir Shipton, slapping him on the back as he dismounts.

'Er, er, yeah. I'm g-glad you th-thought s-s-so, S-s-sir Sh-sh-shipton,' he replies and then, shakily, goes to sit down on a fallen tree trunk.

'Yes, nothing like a terrifying ride through Worm Mountain to get your blood pumping,' rattles on Sir Shipton.

'Yeah, one of 'em could've burrowed in at any moment, from any direction, to trap us in the tunnel,' cuts in Sir Angost and with dramatic emphasis draws out the last part of the sentence, 'and they always come in pairs.'

'I am surprised they didn't react to the thunderous noise of our passage. We would have represented quite a meal for them,' pipes in Sir Veneric matter of factly, destroying the suspense and any further comments aimed at Sir Trepid. He then goes on pondering, inaudibly. All eyes are on him, waiting for something more. He notices and decides to offer another philosophical suggestion, 'We will need to travel back through the mountain. I wonder if they will be waiting.'

Silence.

Only Sir Jovien is able to think of something to break it. His deep, booming voice, suddenly, opens up in cheerful song,

'Behold the brave warriors,
Who have laughed upon Death.
We hope not to tempt him,
So we hope that he's deaf.
Ha, haa, ha, haa,
Ha, ha, ha, ha, haa.
Ha…'

'Shhh, for ... for ... for anyone's sake, shh,' whispers Sir Prancealot, loudly and harshly. 'The aliens will hear your voice echoing down on them. And, we do want this to be a surprise attack, don't we!?!' He flicks his head round to stare at Yalwas Phypa, who had begun to harmonise with Sir Jovien.

Once everyone is quiet, he starts talking about a battle plan in the same harsh whisper. By the time he has drawn a crude map of the complex in the dirt with a twig, Pseudomin and Zaly Stabard arrive at a gallop. Pseudomin is screaming and Zaly Stabard has his ears flat back and eyes wide in terror. The knights and horses part, making way, and the map is destroyed. Only hoof prints remain.

The horses chuckle, quietly. The knights stand silent, not wishing to provoke Sir Prancealot's wrath. After a while Sir

Curidge ventures to say something, 'I'll go get him, bring him back.'

'I'll go with him. We'll find him quicker together,' suggests Sir Shipton.

'I'll go, too,' chimes in Sir Hardgrip.

'They could use me, as well,' says Sir Angost.

'I think it would be best if I were to join them,' whispers Sir Veneric. 'It appears he has met with a worm and will need calming down.'

'You know what they say, "many eyes and ears make short work of a treasure hunt," jokes Sir Jovien as he pulls himself into the saddle.

'Can, can ... will it b-be alright, alright if, if I-I go?' asks Sir Trepid, timorously. He accepts no answer as confirmation of his request and he rides off with the others. You are left alone with Sir Prancealot.

A very strange look has come across his face. His head seems to be swelling, ready to explode. He starts making violent gestures toward the dirt and strange grunting, spitting, hissing noises. He struts around the spot he is cursing, waving his arms in the air and pronouncing words in a foreign language with explicit vehemence. Sir Prancealot, for a finale, falls to his knees and weeps into his hands.

He is using words that you recognise and understand, now, 'Damn, damn, damn and bloody hell. I overlooked the two guardhouses. The whole plan is completely, bloody, useless, anyway.' The sobbing is quite disconcerting. No one likes to see a knight cry.

Pseudomin is also sobbing when you find him. He is laying over Zaly Stabard who is asleep. You slide down from the back of Rhad Sa Lanis and Sir Prancealot, gracefully, jumps off after you.

'Come now. Come now, Pseudomin. It's all over now. We're here to protect you. Have you seen the others?' Sir Prancealot says in an uncharacteristically soft tone.

'No. No, I haven't,' Pseudomin splutters in response. He goes on to wail, 'It almost got us. A gigantic, white worm. Zaly wouldn't run until he saw it. It chased us, chased us right out the mountain. And it kept coming. It kept coming. It wanted to eat me,' he whimpers, moans and then bursts into tears, again. A rustle from the bushes sends Pseudomin further into hysteria. He babbles and screams, shouting, 'It's coming to get me. It's coming to get me.'

Sir Prancealot jumps up and over to the area, sword in hands. He calls back a moment later, 'Don't fret, it's only Micalwish Nutear, the Captain's horse returned.' You then hear him ask, 'Have a nice wander, Mici? Where are the others?'

'They went on ahead, like you planned, to cause a diversion so you and the Captain could slip in to the main building. So, you'd best hurry up if you're going to get there before nightfall,' she answers, tartly.

Dodging raised roots and hanging branches, you all scamper down a rocky and muddy path between the trunks of the conifer trees. The horses lead, Sir Prancealot follows behind Zaly Stabard, desperately trying to motivate him to move faster. Pseudomin walks awkwardly, holding up his robe from the ground so as not to dirty it and you consistently bump into him each time he pauses to jump over a puddle.

After what seems like hours, you see the river. It has been out of view since the party came below the treeline. You stand at the water's edge, knee deep in bracken and ivy, looking over the rapidly moving expanse, observing no way of overcoming the obstacle. On the other side lies your objective, towering into the sky amongst the backdrop of mountains, a huge white dome with grey blocks spreading out from beneath it. To the right of them, further down the valley, you see the two massive spacecraft, terrifying despite being dormant.

Sir Prancealot has stepped into the water and is searching for something hidden in the underbrush. With mighty swings, he hacks through the tangle of vegetation, devastating a large area before finding what he was looking for. A sudden thump defines its location and his sword is lodged, firmly, into a felled tree trunk that had been concealed. Sir Prancealot heaves his sword free and then rips the flora away to uncover a raft.

'We have many of these rafts dotted along the banks of this river. We use them to patrol our border,' he explains to you. 'The horses will have to stay behind, so you'd best take what you need from them, while I get this into the river.'

As far as Mici is concerned, this is the end of the mission and she hurries you to take the load from her back and allow her to wander along the riverbank, before it gets too dark to see anything. You check your equipment: laser rifle, explosives, detonator, radio, combat knife, flare gun, rope, grappling hooks and provisions. Pseudomin is engaged in the same activity, though he is packing his equipment into a small box: large leather-bound spell books, jars of herbs and bits of animals, stones, bags of dust, rods, staves, orbs and biscuits.

Sir Prancealot comes back up the bank only to take a spear and provisions from Rhad Sa Lanis.

With only quiet, reserved goodbyes, the three of you embark across the river, Sir Prancealot piloting, using a paddle over the rear of the craft to steer. In a hushed voice he goes through the details of the plan for the last time, the new, revised plan due to his oversight with the original one. You are now going to attempt to destroy the generator building on the river, rather than the radar installation itself. That way the security and surveillance systems will also be disabled and the other knights would have a chance to create the diversion, without being noticed and decimated before reaching the intended target between two guard posts. The risk for yourselves is being caught in the explosion, but, in the case of survival, the three of you will go on to infiltrate the complex through the causeway entrance.

The river is rushing you away, downstream, heading for the grey block building, held above the water on stilts made of the same matt-grey material. With careful scrutiny you can see beneath the construction, the water is swirling in a circular motion, drawing the river's flow toward it. This does not disrupt the river, however, which happily continues its course through the tree-lined valley, en route to the distant, open sea, presently obscured by mountains.

Pseudomin grips, tightly, to the bindings that hold the raft together, screaming how he does not want to die, each time the white-water spray leaps over the raft as it dips and jumps in rhythm with the river. Sir Prancealot stands, legs wide, one hand on hip the other controlling the paddle. He seems motionless in his glistening, silver armour, unperturbed by the turbulence or the danger. You sit carefully preparing the explosives and setting the detonator. You concentrate on flipping through the display of red letters and numbers, instead of the turmoil around you to avoid feeling sick.

'Are you ready, Captain?' shouts Sir Prancealot. 'I'll aim us for the nearest stilt and tie the raft to it to stop us going in that whirlpool. We'll have to find a way in from there, we'll never get away from the pull of that thing.'

You pull one of the ropes from your backpack and carefully uncoil it a little and then tie the loose end to the bindings at the rear of the raft.

'I hope it holds,' yells Sir Prancealot. 'I'm going to try jamming us between those two posts there. The ones close together, you see? Do you think you can get the rope around the one on the right?'

Night comes, suddenly, without warning. The entire valley is in the shadow of the mountain range. The water is so opaque it almost appears to be solid, only the motion of it convinces you otherwise. The black shapes of buildings help you to distinguish the shore from the river, it is a long way off and the enormous tube connecting the generator to the complex stretches the entire distance.

Faster and faster, brazenly onwards, carried by the roaring, angry river. You lose sight of the structure for a moment, then it is there before you and the impact tosses you forward, under the building and into the whirlpool. You cling to the rope; using all of your strength and willpower to resist the swirling river's. You are tugged and twisted, beaten and bruised at the mercy of this phenomenon, though barely aware of it. Only the rope is real. It twitches and pulls. Around and around you spin, trying to catch a breath with each surface. You are near the raft. It is jammed, with precision, between the two posts that Sir Prancealot had aimed for. You see him reaching hand over hand, reeling you in. Pseudomin is in a state of excited confusion, not knowing what to hold on to, how to help nor why he was screaming when he is not the one in trouble. On the raft behind them is a figure you can scarcely make out: a black horse's shape, with wings folded and eyes that you recognise. The rope slips from your grasp and you wind around the rim of the whirlpool and then you are taken down into its spiralling depths.

Flowing water is drumming on something hollow and you hear a clock chime from the other room.

'I'll kill you. I'll kill you, you shit-bag. You stinking shit!'

You lift yourself from the tiled floor and watch her for her next move. Blood pumps from the wound in her stomach but, she seems to feel no pain and she is unconcerned by it. The dress and the lower half of her cardigan are saturated and red droplets are sprayed with each of her feigning movements. She waves the knife at you and stares, insanely, with her bulbous eyes, making odd expressions with her pale, sweaty face and rolling her pointed tongue, slowly and grotesquely, around her thin, cracked lips, drooling and gurgling.

She screeches out a laugh and then hisses, 'I'll make you regret it. Yes, I will. I'll teach you a lesson you'll never forget.' With the last two words she suddenly lunges at you, screaming fiercely as you catch her and manage to keep the knife from yourself. You struggle, huffing and grunting, being pushed right back over the work surface, just missing the cupboards above with your head. The woman gives up trying to plunge the knife into your chest and instead has taken to biting at your neck. In an unexpected frenzy, you succeed in shoving her away from you, she hits the floor and the knife goes free, sliding to a halt at the far wall, under the mirror.

The woman wipes her mouth on her sleeve, glances over at the knife and then stares back at you. She bears her rotting teeth and vocalises an inhuman noise from her throat. Her eyes roll and she launches herself, off the wall, at you. Stepping aside, instinctively, you let her smash into the racks of plates and cutlery, spreading the fragments all along the work surface. She flops and lies motionless, her head amidst shards of white porcelain. With a sense of urgency, you recover your wits and retrieve the knife. She stirs, slowly, shaking the pieces of broken plate from her hair. In desperation she clutches at the work surface, in vain. She, unable to stop herself falling, slides sideways, her left leg buckling beneath her, reaching out over the sideboard, hugging it tightly to hold herself up.

Something you cannot hear at first, the woman is muttering, but the volume of her voice rises with her anger and disbelief and she is soon shouting, repetitiously, with hopeless obscenity, 'You fucker. You fuck-ker, you shit. You fucking shit-bag.' She sustains each word, emphasising her hatred and head-butts the sideboard between each syllable. Then your reflexes make you run toward her. She has the cup and saucer in each hand, threatening to throw them at you. The cup catches you on the chin, the saucer has slipped from her hand in her haste to throw it at you, bounced off the window to smash back onto the sideboard. Momentarily stunned, you stand, staring at the floor where the cup lay broken.

Taking advantage of your state, the woman rushes you, again. This you anticipated. You grab her hair, as you step to one side, and then run her into the mirror on the far wall, face first. You immediately release her to cover yourself from flying glass but only numerous cracks appear and the mirror remains intact and firmly attached to the wall. She lies slumped and groaning on the floor at your feet. You begin to move away, stepping backwards over her sprawling legs. A lightbulb dangles shadeless and lonely in the middle of the sandy-white ceiling. The floor meets the back of your head with a crack and, after the brief vision loss, you see she has moved, quickly, and her face is only inches from yours. She is smiling, flashing her eyes and blinking with timidity.

'You know I love you, really,' she says in a soppy, appealing tone, running the fingers of her right hand, gently, over your scalp. 'I don't want to hurt you and I know you don't want to hurt me.' She is laying all her weight on you, balancing on her elbows set either side of your head. 'Let go of the knife and we'll be friends, again. Go on, don't you want us to be friends?'

She is impatient for an answer and suddenly jerks herself up into a kneeling position, her hands wrapped firmly around your neck. The strength in her fingers is incredible. You cannot catch a breath. You try rolling, flipping, twisting and pulling but every second of struggling brings you closer to death.

'Let go of the knife and I'll stop. We can be friends, again.'

You are choking. You feel as if your face will burst. In desperation you drive the knife into her stomach, again, and feel the warm blood spill onto your hand and body. She stops, rigid, with her hands still clasped around your throat. Her eyes stare blankly, her whole expression is one of utter astonishment. You roughly wrench the blade out and attempt to wriggle out from under her. This just snaps her back to attention. She resumes her strangulating hold and begins to raise and smash down your head, raise and … you thrust again, through her rib-cage, you notice the sensation of blade scraping bone all up your arm. She coughs. Chokes. And then blood streams from between her lips, dripping onto your face. She only pauses, before lifting your head, again. Crack.

You are fighting blind, stabbing and slashing, choking and kicking and, finally, she is off and you can breathe. After four or five deep breaths your sight returns. She is slumped, face down, over your legs, still on her knees. You kick her off and she falls, lifeless, over backwards, to strike her head against the far wall. Her open eyes seem to stare at you but they are dead-eyes, the spirit that shined in them has gone. The knife stands upright in the centre of her chest as testimony to the fact. A thick pool is rapidly growing around her, everything else is still. But, there is a hollow drumming sound and ... and the sound of splashing water. From the other room, you can hear the relentless ticking of a clock and outside an aeroplane drones across the sky.

You wobble to a stand and head to the front door of the apartment wanting to get away as quickly as possible. Reconsidering your impulsive decision you redirect yourself to the sink to wash some of this blood from yourself first. The clear, pure liquid pounds on the plastic, green and white bottle before running its course to the plug-hole. You prop yourself against the sink and watch the water whirl around and around in a declining circle to oblivion.

BEYOND THE BOUNDS

'Captain. Captain. Are you in one piece? We're inside, it's alright. Pseudomin actually got a spell right and managed to magic us in here. Good job, eh?' Sir Prancealot holds onto your arm while you climb to your feet and then turns to say to Pseudomin, 'Well done, very well done indeed. This was a fine time to get one right. Now, we just need to plant the explosives and infiltrate the compound.'

You look about the room. This is definitely a control room of some kind, with flashing displays and touch-sensitive panels and a machine in the centre, glowing with a weird green intensity. There are no windows to this room and the sliding metal door is circular and gigantic. The floor is slippery, covered with an oily residue which smells, convincingly, like stale urine. The dim illumination emanates from a series of blue lamps, arranged in the shape of a triangle in the ceiling.

'So, where's our dunnage?' asks Sir Prancealot, after a rapid search of the room.

'Sorry,' answers Pseudomin, 'I was so concerned with saving us that I forgot all about the equipment.'

'Oh, for Bobbabin's sake! How are we going to stop this thing, now. So much for getting a spell right for the first time,' exclaims Sir Prancealot, throwing his hands in the air.

'Well, I got it half right, at least. It would have been worse if I'd saved the bags and left us to the mercy of the whirlpool,' replies Pseudomin, meekly, in his own defence. He then adds, 'I was, actually, trying to levitate the Captain out of the whirlpool, but, somehow I thought about it too much and we all ended up in here.'

Sir Prancealot is stomping about the room, slipping occasionally but maintaining balance and dignity. He suddenly stops and sighs deeply. 'I suppose we'll just have to do this the old fashioned way. See if you can open that door while I figure out how hard to hit this thing.' He walks over to the glowing, green machine and begins to tap on the metal surfaces with his metal gloved fist.

Pseudomin tugs at your sleeve; you go over to the door with him and inspect the panel, on the wall, beside it. The symbols and shapes are bewildering, flashing all colours of the spectrum and giving no clue as to which is the correct button to press. Pseudomin's baffled expression confirms that he expects you to accomplish the task.

'Ah, ha!' cries out Sir Prancealot. He has managed to prise the metal plating from one side of the machine and has revealed the complex circuitry inside. The plate covered an area the size of a normal doorway and Sir Prancealot has guided its fall to the floor and it now provides a non-slippery platform for him to stand on. He stares at the boards and components as though figuring out what does what and how to disrupt it. You turn your attention back to the panel.

There are twelve patches of shifting colour, you presume them to be buttons, arranged in rows, with a small display screen flashing unfamiliar icons and letters above them. One button, larger than the rest, sits at the bottom of the panel, lighting up green then blue alternately. Guessing that this is the most likely button to release the lock, you impulsively press it. From within the wall, there is a sudden loud sound like that of air being forced from a pressurised bottle and the massive, metal door begins to slowly shift aside.

'Ah, well done, Captain,' calls over Sir Prancealot. 'I believe this contraption is an integral part of the generator. If I destroy the strange bits and pieces in this,' he points into the buzzing machine, 'it may stop the whole, damn thing.' He draws his sword from the scabbard on his back and prepares to make a mighty thrust into the heart of the machine. 'Go out and check that the way is clear. We'll need to find a route into the main complex.'

Pseudomin needed no further encouragement and he quickly peeks his head through the doorway. 'Looks clear to me,' he says, before stepping out, dragging you by your sleeve behind him.

The exit leads into a tubular corridor, with the same slime and weird, blue lighting. At the end is another sliding door and an identical panel beside it. A snap, fizz and pitiful yelp sounds from the control room and suddenly you are in complete darkness. You both rush back to Sir Prancealot. He is motionless. Paralysed. Blue sparks of electricity ripple all over his armour; his arms are outstretched, gripping the conductive metal sword in both hands and he stands on the metal plate on the slime-covered metal floor.

'Well, that was pretty stupid,' Pseudomin states, remorselessly.

The green light intensifies along with the horrible humming noise. The machine has been disrupted. The same blue streaks of electricity run through the displays and other panels and the room is filling, fast, with thick, black smoke.

'Do you think it will explode?' Pseudomin asks you, tugging at your sleeve. He does not wait for an answer, he turns and tries to run down the corridor.

You chase after him, helping him up after his fall half way along. You struggle to run together and simultaneously smack, blindly, into the sealed, circular, sliding door. The panel's display no longer flashes, the buttons are colourless and none of them seems to activate anything, regardless of how hard you both bash them. The hum progresses into a whine and the green light is now enough to see by. You appeal to Pseudomin to cast a spell or something, just as long as he gets it right. He agrees to try. He takes a step back and begins to gyrate and incant. He looks like he is attempting to do a popular children's dance but cannot remember the words, the tune or the motions. The whine has now become a whistle and the light is almost blinding you.

The door jerks aside. Stops. Jerks a little more, stops, shudders, slides away and immediately slides shut, again. Open, shut, open, shut, open and so on and not slowly.

'Sorry. It's the best I can do in these conditions,' apologises Pseudomin. 'I'll try to jump through first, if you like.'

The smoke is gathering around you and you will soon be unable to see when it is a good time to jump or not. You nod at Pseudomin and his face drops in despair. He readies himself, hesitates and leaps like a drunk frog through the portal just managing to miss having his ankles crushed. You take a deep breath and watch the gap, timing the period it is there for. Open, shut, open, shut, you launch yourself with all your strength, open, you land in a crumpled heap on Pseudomin, shut. You permit yourself a sigh of relief. There is an almighty explosion and you spin your head to see the surge of fire racing at the portal. You scurry to one side, dragging Pseudomin with you, and the metal fragments of the door are blasted past you. But the heat sears against your flesh and you are both knocked into the air to land, heavily, upon the slime-coated floor.

This massive chamber is illuminated by several small fires, which are dotted about in no particular pattern. The spinning column, going through a hole in the floor in the centre of the chamber, is grinding to a halt and by looking over the railings you can see down to the river, into the decreasing whirlpool. The fires do not cast their light high enough for you to see the ceiling, but you can make out the walkway around, and the two other exits on this level. Another circular, sliding door covers the exit opposite the control room but the other is wide open. It is the main tube that crosses over the river to the complex on the shore. Beyond the tunnel entrance you cannot distinguish anything but darkness. Pseudomin is scrabbling around the wreckage, picking up the odd shard of metal, scrutinising it for a moment, then discarding it until he comes across a metal pole, bent to an acute angle two-thirds along its length. He stamps repeatedly upon it, bringing it nearer to being straight and then stands with it, outstretched, in one hand. He performs another dance with peculiar lyrics and the end of the pole, furthest from his hand, springs into life, irradiating a soft, pure, white light.

'The Light Spell was the first spell I learned and is the only one I get right every time,' Pseudomin tells you with pride.

He hands you the pole and waits for you to lead the way into the tube.

You are both absolutely saturated with the unpleasantly aromatic slime and you have hardly progressed a hundred metres down the tube-way. The pole illuminates to a short distance ahead of you, but your hearing extends much further. You hear metal grating on metal, the sound that a rusty garage door makes when it is opening. Pseudomin has noticed the sound too and has begun to whimper in panic. You hastily lower the tip of the torch into the oily residue, plunging yourselves into relative darkness and then you grab Pseudomin by the arm and head back the way you just came. The grating stops, but the echoes linger on.

Just as you are entering the main chamber, again, you start to hear it. A peculiar slurping sound, growing louder very, very quickly. Whatever is creating the noise is right behind you and you dive to the side as you exit the tunnel. An alien snail beast stands metres above you, all of its tendrils wriggle and twitch with agitation. The firelight glistens upon its moist, spongy skin, making it appear even more revolting and fearsome. Pseudomin has reverted to speaking gibberish and having spasms. The alien slides effortlessly forward stretching out its tentacle arms to grab you. A puff of smoke and a large naked woman falls heavily on top of you both.

You manage to writhe yourself free; Pseudomin, though, has been smothered. The woman does not move. She seems to be stunned. From underneath her, you can hear muffled cries for help and you notice fingertips waving from her right armpit. Levering yourself beneath her shoulder, you lift, stagger, push, slip, groan and, finally, succeed in rolling her over. Pseudomin lays there, crushed and winded. He stares up at the at the unseeable ceiling, blinking infrequently, waiting for the feeling to come back to his body. She also stares straight up, blinking occasionally, wearing an expression of total astonishment. They lay side by side looking as though they have just had the most amazing night of their lives.

Mouthing the words, with uncertainty, she asks, 'What, what happened? What have you done to me?' Unfamiliar and awkward, she forces herself to sit up and then she studies the new form she has. 'I, I, I look like you! One of you!? Vermin. Parasite. Disease ... How? ... How did you do this?' She shakes Pseudomin roughly and he sits up instantly and looks all around himself, coming to rest his focus on the alien woman. 'Why did you do this? How? How?' she demands, pushing him to emphasise her distress.

'I don't know,' he replies, pleadingly. 'I don't know. I was trying to teleport myself home. I'm sorry, I'm sorry, please stop hitting me.'

'Change me back! Change me back, NOW!' she shouts.

'I, I can't. I don't know how. I haven't learned any spells concerning metamorphosis and I haven't got a clue how to change humans into giant alien snails,' Pseudomin rants out, hurriedly, with a squeak of fear in his voice.

'You must, you must, you must!' she screams, pounding him with the flat of her hands, adding the odd karate chop to the neck and slap around the face.

You run over to intervene, persuading her to calm down by stating the obvious: that he will be unable to do anything if she kills him.

'Agh!' she utters as though pained. 'So, you call yourselves human. We call you infestation.'

'W-why?' asks Pseudomin, fearfully.

'This planet is rare. It can sustain life and has plenty of water. You humans destroy it. If you are not eradicated, this planet and everything on it will die.'

'Oh,' responds Pseudomin, as though enlightened.

'We have studied your species. We have been ordered to begin the atmospheric conversion process. Soon, the conditions will be right for our invasion force to land. We will eliminate you all and then repair the damage you have done to this world.' She climbs onto her knees, using Pseudomin as a prop. 'You have stopped the generator. How?'

'Well ... well, er ... Sir, Sir Prancealot put his sword in your, your green machine thing,' Pseudomin hesitantly answers.

'Agh! If that is damaged it could take time to fix. Come with me. You will assist with the repairs.'

'Well, actually ... we, we're here to rescue the people you abducted.'

'You cannot. You will assist me,' she commands in an unwavering tone.

Pseudomin suddenly jerks himself away, rolls to his feet and stands up. The alien woman, without a prop, falls flat on her face, not sparing a twitch to save herself. 'No. I want to save my countrymen and allies,' he states, while waggling his finger at her, 'and, you will do what I tell you or I'll turn you into ... into ... into a loaf of bread and eat you,' he declares with uncharacteristic authority. 'Now, stand up and take us to where you are holding them.'

It takes her several attempts to stand and keep her balance and only then with the aid of yourself and Pseudomin, one under each arm. The tube, to the main complex, goes on forever. At the speed you are going, it will probably take you twice as long to get there. Slipping, stumbling, collapsing and continuously grasping at thin air you all persevere, as conjoined triplets, towards an exit you cannot yet see.

'Is it going to be like this all the way?' asks Pseudomin, between puffs.

'Yes. In my proper form I would be able to move faster than the fastest of your species while on this surface. It is difficult controlling this human body. I am amazed that you can move anywhere. This one step after another is inefficient and tiring. This frame is fragile and has no protection. I am in pain everywhere for these falls. I cannot understand how you can exist like this,' she replies, spitting the words out in contempt.

'Well, I s'pose we're born like it and just get used to it after a while,' remarks Pseudomin, 'And in return, I can't see the benefits of being a giant snail. I bet your balls are, really, dull and boring. You can hardly fox-trot or jive with that massive shell on your back.'

'What are you talking about?' she asks, angry and perplexed.

'Dancing. You know, dancing. Moving your body to music.'

'No.'

'Remind me to show you sometime. You'll be able to learn, now that you've got a body that can do it. I'll teach you the lambada or the salsa, something exciting,' offers Pseudomin, ignoring her hostility.

He then goes on to explain all the dances he knows and tries to hum the tunes that they would be done to. The alien woman has started showing a keen interest in what he is saying and stops from time to time to try some of the movements. After suffering a painful fall attempting the Twist, they decide to change the topic of conversation to ecology. Pseudomin listens, intently, while she explains the alien's method of reforming planets, so that they provide life-supporting environments. She then goes on to say that human beings are the first race that they have encountered that is actively trying to destroy its own world. All the other races in the galaxy are terrified about human beings succeeding in their pitiful attempts to travel into space and searching for new habitable planets. All the aliens had genuinely thought that humans were a planetary infestation and a serious threat to other worlds. Earth has been quarantined since it was discovered. It has only been observed from a great distance, no space traffic has passed near and no vessel, until now, has been allowed to land. The aliens had abducted individuals so as to restrict the chances of contamination. They found that they could not communicate with the specimens they had taken, nor did they recognise intelligent behaviour in them. On this evidence, the Galactic Council concluded that the human species was a deadly, planetary plague that needed to be combated before it consumed the Earth and spread into the galaxy.

'Oh, dear,' is Pseudomin's, shocked, response to her story, 'I had no idea that humans have travelled into space.'

'You have not. Not, in any effective sense. The attempts have been futile. A small bunch of you made it to the barren satellite in orbit of your planet. Another group launched themselves into orbit to assemble bits of metal into a shape we do not understand, to do nothing we can comprehend, and since then you have just been firing metal boxes at the other planets in your system. One went astray and judging by the symbols we found on it, we presumed it to be a warning buoy,' explains the alien woman.

Her arm is constricting around your neck like a hungry python and the stench from the slime and her armpit is making you faint. You have not got a clue how far you still have to go, for all the steps, slips and tumbles you have taken, there is no change in the scenery. The metallic walls still curl up and over you and the darkness is still as obscuring.

'So, what is your home world like?' Pseudomin asks her, after a long period of silence.

'There is more moisture in the air. The average temperature, over the whole planet, is much higher. The vegetation grows, even, on the poles and we have no deserts. The surface is divided, equally, between land and water, though the seas are shallower and the land flatter. Our planet has a much closer orbit to our star, which is larger and releases less intense radiation. The atmosphere is similar. Our magnetic field is thirty times more powerful and our ozone layer is intact,' she replies in a matter of fact manner.

'Don't you have any moons?' queries Pseudomin, deeply curious.

'No. We presume our star's gravity pulled them away from our planet when our system was first forming. There are several small planetoids orbiting between our star and our world.'

'How long did it take for you to get here?' continues Pseudomin in his questioning.

'I do not know how to answer. It took one-twentieth of my expected life-span,' she says, puzzled. Pseudomin is also puzzled and remains quiet, for a while, considering her reply.

The three of you are adapting to the conditions in the tube-way. You can see further and keep your balance better. You all slide along using a crude ice-skating action, as if you were taught by a beginner skiing instructor on brown mush instead of white ice. The alien woman is now insisting that she needs to rest; her legs are numb and refusing to operate. Pseudomin remains assertive and tells her that there will be no resting until the prisoners are free and everyone has escaped, safely.

'You will not escape,' she states, bluntly. 'The others will come to find out why the power has not been restored.'

'Not if my comrades are keeping them busy, they won't,' retorts Pseudomin. 'Besides, they would have come by now, if they were coming at all. There seems to be no end to this tunnel and we've been in here for ages.'

The alien does not answer. The sound of their chatter falls away, leaving the huffs, puffs and groans echoing from the walls. On and on and on in near silence. Then, there it is. The doorway to the main complex. Still open from when the alien opened it. You are both dragging her along, but you manage to quicken the pace, despite her bulk.

Finally there, you peep either way into absolute darkness. You can just make out the corridor forming a T-junction with this tube-way, the curved wall opposite looks exactly like every other piece of curved wall you've seen so far.

'Which way now?' Pseudomin asks the alien.

'That way,' she answers, pointing right.

On and on, again, you go, through endless slimy tubing and the more you progress, the more you are convinced that these are sewage tunnels and that there will be a fresh surge of wet filth coming at you any minute. Another intersection. You go left, another and you turn right. You pass two doors, staggered on either side of the tube-way. More metal tunnel and then a massive reinforced door at the end.

'The specimens are behind this door. Two of them were taken to isolation because they were uncontrollable. They are behind the two doors we passed,' the alien tells you. 'Now, I must rest,' she says, flopping to the floor like a melting jelly.

'How do we get it open?' asks Pseudomin, after staring at it for a while.

'That is your problem,' replies the alien, in a flat, lethargic tone.

'Maybe we should try to open the other two doors first,' suggests Pseudomin to you, 'the people behind them might be able to help us force this one open, and you,' he turns to the alien woman and continues, 'can help us.'

She sighs, heavily, with no intention of moving a muscle. Then, in a defeated voice, she says, 'The emergency door release mechanism is behind the panel. You will need to smash the panel to get at it. The main panel for this door is in the guard room at the other end of this corridor, but there is normally a guard on duty in there.'

Pseudomin rubs his chin in thought. He frowns and squints and bites his lip before saying, 'Well, that could make things difficult. But if I can turn you into one of us I'm sure I can turn the guard into a goldfish or something harmless. First, let's get these other two out.'

Pseudomin leads the way back to the two doors leaving the alien woman to rest in darkness, her heavy breaths keeping you aware of her whereabouts. He steps out of the way, allowing you to take a swing at the first panel. You hit it with the handle end of the glowing pole and it shatters easily, showering a glasslike substance over you. Revealed is a lever. You tug upon and it eventually gives and you hear the sound of pressurised air being released. With a determined shove the door rolls aside.

From inside the voice of a woman says, 'Bloody hell, am I glad to see you. I was starting to think I would be spending forever in here.' Cassandra Banks steps into the light, her stern face almost bearing a smile. She still wears the black army uniform, burned away in places, and the cap sits firmly on her head, covering the blond, spiky hair.

She anticipates your questions and begins to give you a brief explanation. 'I was hurt bad by the blast, but I was not dead when they found me. I remember being in a tank of some sort, floating in an antiseptic solution, with tubes and needles sticking in me everywhere. I was unconscious most of the time. When I came fully around I was completely healed and they put me in with the other prisoners. They put me in isolation when I got caught trying to help the others escape. I don't think they got very far, they kept slipping on the slime and didn't have a clue which way to go.' Cassandra steps into the tube-way, steadies herself, looks both ways and then turns to you and asks, 'How did you get in here? I hope your escape plan is better than mine was. And who's this guy?'

You answer her questions, with equal brevity, and then introduce her to Pseudomin.

'Lovely to meet you, Sergeant Banks. Can you help us to open the other doors?', Pseudomin asks her, hurriedly. He seems to be getting nervous again, reverting back to his familiar timid self.

'I can help you,' she confirms, 'But, what you want to ask me is *will* I help you.'

'Er ... er, yes. W-will you help us?' Pseudomin repeats, shocked by her statement. He shyly looks away and then tries to stride over to the next door, but instead he slips and looks like he is auditioning for the National Ballet Troop, finishing with the splits and a pained expression.

You leave Cassandra to help him up, while you smash the panel to the next door and pull on the lever. The three of you tug at the door and it rolls open. It is dark and not a sound comes from within. You step inside and the light from the pole fills the curved, metallic-walled room. An old man lies face down on the floor to the left of you. He stirs as you gently shake him to see if he is alive.

'It's about bloody time. I've been here bloody ages. One minute on the Evening Star free as a fish in the sea, the next you and Jess have pissed off and left me to the mercy of these bloody aliens. Buggered off and left me you did. The least you could've done was come and get me sooner. They've been mistreating me something horrible. I kept telling them that humans cannot live on lettuce alone but they wouldn't bloody listen to me, would they. No, they just slurp and gurgle at you, make a few curious, rude looking gestures and then bring you another enormous plate of bloody lettuce. Monsters. That's what they are, bloody monsters. Who are these people?'

Pseudomin and Cassandra have stepped through the doorway, startling the Old Man, causing him to shake visibly. You introduce them as co-rescuers and tell him their names. You then explain the general situation, remembering to mention that you have an alien captive. The Old Man does not know whether to be happy or dismayed and you do not give him the time to decide. You hurry, precariously, back to where you have left the alien woman and tell the Old Man to watch her while you, Cassandra and Pseudomin attempt to get the main prison door open from in the guardroom. Pseudomin casts a Light Spell on a piece of broken panel and leaves it, in the yellowy-green slime, on the floor. It radiates it's light like that of a small camp fire, though unflickering and eerie.

'You can't leave me here with this, this naked woman,' The Old Man says, his voice raising with anxiety.

'Shhh.'

'You'll have all the aliens in the base descending upon us, if you're not quiet,' chastises Cassandra in a harsh whisper.

'You don't have to worry about her trying to escape,' Pseudomin assures him. 'She's too tired to move now, after the long walk here. I doubt she'll give you any trouble. If she wakes up, tell her that I'm within shouting distance and I will fly back to cast another spell on her, something really unpleasant.'

'Well if you're such a bloody good magician, magic her some clothes to wear. It would be indecorous to leave her like this,' chides the Old Man.

Pseudomin appears to be stunned by the challenge. He stares blankly at the Old Man, at the alien, back at the Old Man, again.

'Come on. This won't be much of a rescue if we all get caught,' states Cassandra with authority.

Pseudomin gathers his wits and says, 'Alright, alright. I'm just trying to think of the right words.' He removes his hat and scratches his head vigorously before replacing it. He then begins to pace in a slow circle, crouching erratically and waving his arms in a close imitation of a chicken. A pause. Wild movement of the arms, whilst reciting gibberish and jogging on the spot. A flash of white light and the incantation is complete. Pseudomin takes a moment to recover his breath while you all gawk at the alien woman's new garment.

'That's a bloody tent,' declares the Old Man after a period of waiting for someone to say something.

'Er ... yes. I didn't get it quite right, did I? I was trying to imagine something in her size,' explains Pseudomin. 'If you take the poles out, you should be able to wrap it around her quite nicely.'

'It will have to do. You can buy her something nice when we've got away from here. So, let's get on with it,' commands Cassandra, her impatience plain in her tone and expression.

Even on this slippery surface Cassandra moves with graceful dexterity. She speeds ahead, only pausing to let you and Pseudomin catch up because you are the one with the torch. You all pause at the intersection, look left and right into darkness and then go straight across, as directed by the alien. At the end of this tube-way is the door to the guardroom, already open. Cassandra and Pseudomin step back to let you lead into the room, as you are the only one carrying anything resembling a weapon, though it is unlikely to cause much damage to an armoured, technologically advanced lifeform ten times your size. The room, however, is empty. In the walls there are consoles with dark, blank displays, the monitors are blank and there is only one panel which is beside the doorway, already smashed. There are no other exits.

'Well, how do we get the prison door open, then?' demands Cassandra.

'Er, the alien said there would be a panel in here which opens it,' replies Pseudomin, with a tremor of uncertainty.

'There isn't a panel here. Not one that isn't already smashed. And there's no guard, either. It seems like she's trying to trick you, to me,' says Cassandra.

'Trick us? But, why would she do that?' Pseudomin asks her, perplexed by the possibility.

'To buy herself time,' answers Cassandra. 'She's hoping that we will be delayed long enough for her buddies to turn up. It's the sort of thing I would do if I were in her position.'

'So, how do we get that door open?' he asks, sounding worried.

'All the other doors have a panel beside them, like this one,' she says pointing toward the doorway. 'The prison door probably has a similar one, somewhere, near it.'

You all immediately start to head back, quickening your skating action for fear of the alien's plan being successful. At the intersection you stop. You can hear movement from the tube-way on your left. Cassandra speeds across and you follow her, tugging at Pseudomin's robe to make him do the same. He falls, but you drag him up and continue on.

The Old Man has adapted the tent to fit over the alien woman like a toga. She, presently has her hands above her head while he is wrapping his arms around her waist desperately trying to grab the other end of the guy rope he is using for a belt. 'Help me,' he says as you approach. Cassandra goes to his aid. She takes the ends of the rope and ties a neat little bow.

Pseudomin, however, flares up at the alien, failing to keep his voice to a tame whisper, 'You lied to me,' he accuses her, 'You made us go all the way to the guardroom, where there was no guard and no panel to smash or lever to pull.'

'Yes. I know. So what. What else did you expect me to do?' she says bluntly in response.

'I expect you to tell me how to open this door before I turn you into a golf ball or summon an ice demon to freeze your behind,' hisses Pseudomin, threateningly.

Cassandra and the Old Man step away from the alien woman, having finished dressing her, and she lets her arms drop to her sides with a huff.

'It's over there,' she reveals, pointing toward the floor, to the right of the reinforced door. Above the slime-line you notice the disguised panel, less obvious because the display is dead.

Cassandra picks up the glowing, slime-covered, broken piece of panel and swaps it with you for the pole. 'Pseudomin,' she says, turning to face him, 'Ask her to describe the best route out of here. We'll have to shift as soon as this door is open.'

The alien explains the way to the spacecraft landing area. It is the nearest exit from the building.

'Hurry. Whoever was making that noise back there didn't sound far away,' whispers Pseudomin to you both, after memorising the directions.

'Are you ready?' Cassandra asks you, poising to smash the panel. You nod and she brings down the butt of the pole, viciously, and then clears away the shards to get at the lever. Over her strenuous vocalisation, you hear the hiss and the shunt of the locking mechanism. Together, you heave at the door.

The light does not extend far into the cavernous cell. You can see a few people hiding in shadows, but otherwise it appears to be silent and empty. From back down the tube-way there is a clatter of metal striking metal and a muffled cry. Cassandra instantly covers the 'light' end of the pole with her cap and you put the shard you hold into one of your pockets. The sound of movement continues toward you, followed, a moment later, by the clatter of metal, again.

'Agh, damn this stuff! Somebody turn that light back on.'

'Shhh. Th-they c-c-could b-be aliens, s-s-still g-guarding the p-p-prisoners.'

'That sounds like Sir Jovien and Sir Trepid,' whispers Pseudomin, in your direction.

You take a chance and pull the piece of panel from your pocket and throw it up the tube-way. It lands with a dull splash, barely heard over the exclamations of, 'What the hell was that,' from the two knights, clearly visible to you in the slime-light.

'Oh, thank the ether, it is them!' shouts Pseudomin, joyfully.

'Who, who's there?' calls Sir Trepid from behind Sir Jovien.

Cassandra uncovers the tip of the pole, allowing them to see who you are.

'It's Pseudomin and the Captain. How glad we are to see you both safe and sound,' says Sir Jovien, slowly, approaching on his hands and knees. He resumes talking, after climbing to his feet, in front of you. 'May I be the first to bring you the happy tidings of our victory. We have slain all of our foes and this fortress is now in our hands.'

'You killed them all!?' the alien woman blurts out in horror.

'Well, no. Not all,' answers Sir Jovien, heartily, 'A few made it to one of those flying machines, but, the rest we slaughtered.'

The alien woman looks mortified. Her lips move to say something, but no sound comes forth.

'Yes. It was a magnificent battle. At first we were totally overwhelmed, the two guard towers kept us right back with their magical beams of light and we didn't dare show ourselves from behind the rocks. Then twelve of the snail-beasts came pouring out of the fortress at us, firing their crossbows of lightning bolts. Sir Angost was hit first. Right on the head. We were amazed to see the bolt bounce off his helmet and head straight at one of the guard towers. Then the power shut off and they were trapped outside, with us. We realised that their bolts of lightning couldn't harm us, so, we charged in amongst them. Our swords shattered their shells like hard boiled eggs, ha, ha. Must have given them quite a shock, eh,' Sir Jovien gives himself a moment to laugh. 'Get it, get it?' he asks, wiping his eyes through his visor. 'They may have thrown the lightning bolts, but, we were the ones who gave the shock, ha, ha, ha ...'

The alien woman's jaw has dropped in abhorrent astonishment at his bragging.

Sir Jovien goes on, 'Well anyway, some of them managed to get the fortress gates open while the others fended us off and then they just out ran us on this infernal, greasy ground of theirs.'

The prisoners have started gathering on the other side of the doorway, suspecting that you might be their rescuers.

'Some of them did escape?' asks the alien woman, her voice trembling with remorse and hope.

'Well, they took off, but, then our allies arrived in their flying machines and blasted them out of the sky, ha, ha, ha. This certainly has been a battle worthy of a great song,' replies Sir Jovien with glee.

The alien woman suddenly sobs. She covers her face with her hands but cannot disguise her despair. Her legs no longer able to support her, she crumples to the floor and lies in the slime, her shoulders twitching, involuntarily.

Pseudomin stares at Sir Jovien with contempt and then drops his head in shame. He sits down beside her and gently pats and rubs her arm, attempting to comfort her.

'What?!' says Sir Jovien in response to everyone glaring at him. 'What, what did I do?'

You explain to him, exactly, who she is and about how you got in and disabled the generator. Sir Jovien does not stay stunned by the story for long.

'So, Sir Prancealot is dead?'

You nod.

'He was blown up, you say?'

You nod, again.

'But, he was electrocuted, first?'

Another nod.

'Well, he always did like to make a theatrical show of everything. He would consider that a hero's death,' Sir Jovien says, finally, with a chuckle.

'Excuse me. Are you here to rescue us?' asks a young female, dressed only in a bathrobe, from amongst the crowd on the other side of the doorway.

'Yes, my dear, we certainly are. All of you follow me and I'll lead the way out,' bellows Sir Jovien.

In small groups, huddled together for support, the prisoners file past you. Cassandra stands on the other side of the doorway, helping people with their balance as they step into the tube-way. Everyone moves around Pseudomin and the grief-stricken alien woman without disturbing them. People of all sorts go by; people from all over the world, from every occupation and segment of society. Twenty, then thirty, forty people go by. Fifty, sixty, seventy and they keep coming. You recognise someone from the Hibee Geebie Tribe and you spot Stacey walking beside him, talking on the mobile phone, she does not even acknowledge seeing you, despite your waving.

Cassandra weaves between the flow of escapees, comes over to you and says, indignantly, 'How rude. Stacey didn't even say hello to me, either. She ignores everyone except for the person on the other end of that phone.' You shrug and continue watching the exodus.

There is a commotion in the doorway. A man is trying to squeeze through the people ahead of him, shouting, 'Oi! Oi, you two. You two over there!'

Suddenly, you have a huge pile up on your hands, people being shoved, people slipping over, people shouting, people screaming and the doorway is impassable. Over the pile of fallen people, the original shouting man clambers toward you.

'You two,' he hollers, pointing at yourself and Cassandra, 'stay there, I want to talk to you.'

The crowd has stopped surging from the other side of the door and the people on the floor have started to crawl on their way. Now, out of the throng, you watch the man try to stand and walk toward you. After several falls, he finds a method that works for him: using his arms outstretched, imitating an aeroplane, and taking pigeon steps. As he progresses, further, into the fullness of the light, you can see he is the groceries courier. Cassandra looks at you with an expression of surprise and bewilderment. As soon as he reaches you he demands an explanation for your actions the other morning, when you knocked him over the head and threw him into a pond when he hadn't even asked you for any money. Cassandra speaks up and admits it was her who was to blame and that she will make it up to him by buying him lunch at an excellent restaurant she knows.

SUNRISE

The charming French restaurant hosts an eloquent band of classical musicians, who provide a wonderfully romantic atmosphere. In the centre of the dining table sits a fresh red rose, held up by a slender crystal vase. A unique pattern winds up from its base, it acts like a prism casting a rainbow effect on the pure, white table cloth. The sun is high in the sky and it is bright outside. Over the balcony you can see the prim, colourful sails of boats bobbing on the brilliant blue sea and your attention is drawn much more to their activity than to the conversation you are being subjected to.

Cassandra and Murdock, the groceries delivery courier, are leaning over the table staring into each other's eyes. She gently twists the stem of her glass between the tips of the fingers of her left hand while slowly stroking the bulb of the glass with her right hand, occasionally running her fingernails around the rim. He fidgets, adjusts his tie, shifts his weight, strains to maintain eye contact.

'So, how old are you, Murdock?'

'Well, uhm ... I-I don't like to say. Have a guess.'

'Thirty-six, thirty-seven? I'm sorry. I didn't say something wrong did I?'

'Uhm, no. No, not, not really. I'm twenty-one. Well, since last Tuesday, anyway.'

Cassandra sits motionless, not even blinking. She recovers and blurts out, 'Wow! Tough job. I had no idea.'

'How old are you?'

'Oh, twenty-seven years, three months, fourteen days, two hours and thirty-nine minutes.'

'I love you, Cassandra.'

'I love you, too, Murdock.'

Their smooching blocks your view of the sea and you turn to concentrate on the musicians churning out a selection of sickly love songs in a tortuous fashion.

'Your love comes rolling like a
white-water river,
You are the giver of love
to me.'

The crooning fool, who has stepped onto the stage, cannot sing. His tune defies the melody and his notes avoid the key; though he is trying to compensate with over-expression and dynamic gesturing. The rest of the song will remain unheard, however. At least, until the tuba player decides to help remove his instrument from the singer's mouth. The singer staggers back off of the stage and attempts to ask the couple at the nearest table for assistance, but his words only sound the note of G-flat. A waiter goes to him and then guides him into the foyer.

A few tables away, to your left, beside the front window overlooking the street, you spot Stacey. Around the same table are three people from the Hibee Geebie Tribe questioning the head-chef on how best to prepare escargot. Sitting at another table, to your right, Pseudomin and the alien woman are discussing the rules of golf and the best conditions to play in. During his explanation of what a golf ball is and what is done with it, she suddenly stands up and slaps him.

'You would have turned me into one of them!' she shouts and slaps him, again. 'A golf ball!' Slap. 'I will show you what it is like to be a golf ball,' she screams, slapping him, repeatedly.

'I'm sorry. I'm sorry,' whimpers Pseudomin under this unexpected barrage. 'It's all I could think of at the time.'

The alien woman is still hitting him when the waiter distracts you. 'Telephone, for you,' he says, placing it on the table, in front of you.

'Hello, Captain?' blares the voice of the Commander from the other end of the line. You answer him and allow him to continue. 'Ah, good. Don't worry, I'm not recalling you to duty, just yet. I wanted to let you know that we have retaken the space station and that there is no sign of any alien presence on, or around, Earth. I even had the Astro-Combat team search Neutron Pizza, the Starbright Hotel and the rest of the moon. So, congratulations, Captain. Your mission was a complete success and we have eradicated the alien threat. King Berthold is holding a party at his palace tonight to celebrate our victory. He says he has a special presentation for you and he looks forward to seeing you, again. I'll see you there tonight then, Captain. Nineteen hundred hours.'

'I want a re-match!'

'Well, you can't, bloody, have one. The Captain won fair and square,' the Old Man shouts back.

'Fair! It wasn't fair. I was distracted by that classical music and camera flashing. The spectators, the umpire, the bleeping machine and even the scoreboard were all against me. They put me right off my game,' your neighbour screams whilst storming about the changing room.

'You're only upset because you lost the bet. You accepted the Captain's challenge and have been defeated. Now, you must stick to your word and stop biting peoples' heads off. Count yourself lucky that the Captain didn't take my advice and use a flamethrower on you.'

'But what am I going to do now?' wails your neighbour. 'Biting heads off is what I do, it's my job to be terrifying and murderous. I don't know how to do anything else.'

'I'm sure you'll find something,' the Old Man tells him, reassuringly, 'You could try being a tour guide. I hear they are in high demand these days.'

Your neighbour sits down on one of the benches and sighs, 'Oh, I suppose I can do that, for a while, but next time I'm choosing the game.'

The Old Man laughs and then leaves you both to get changed. With wings and teeth adorned again, the Creature holds open the changing room door and invites you to walk out first.

The ocean stretches out before you; the waves gently lapping up and down the shoreline with a relaxing, unrhythmic repetition. The cool, fresh sea-breeze brushes the excess heat from your skin to leave the soothing warmth of the sun's rays to penetrate and ease your muscles into a state of comfortable lethargy. You recline back into the soft, sweet-smelling grass of the hillside and watch the white, puffy clouds slowly wander through the sky, almost imperceptibly transforming into familiar shapes and figures. You listen to the birds singing from the trees behind you; a harmonic, erratic and pleasant noise, especially when accompanied by the leaves and waves. You lay there naked, but you don't care, because you are completely alone, with the exception of the birds, who definitely don't care. You lay there watching the sun make its steady progress across the light blue sky without a care in the world. This is your island, you can do as you please.

'Well, this world is certainly full of surprises, isn't it?' the Old Man says aloud, attempting to engage in conversation with you. He removes the top hat from his head and carefully brushes the confetti from the brim. 'It has certainly been a lovely day for it. I'm boiling in this outfit.' He replaces his hat and takes off the jacket, to shake it. 'I'm glad I wasn't Sir Curidge, the best man. I would've died in that suit of armour.'

The Old Man does look good in a tuxedo, almost distinguished. You are both standing outside the cathedral, watching the last of the guests leaving, in horse-drawn carriages.

'Jessica looked resplendent in that light blue lace dress of hers, though. It was good of her to leave the sea to be here as Cassandra's bridesmaid. Especially, it being the wrong phase of the moon and all that,' rambles on the Old Man.

You can see Jessica climbing into the carriage at the front of the queue. She waves to you and you return the gesture, then Sir Curidge closes the door behind them and the carriage rolls away.

'I never would have guessed it. Cassandra and that courier,' the Old Man says, apparently disgusted by the thought. 'Pseudomin and the alien woman was in the cards, anyone could tell that they were in love, but Cassandra and that Murdock fellow getting married as well has left me flabbergasted.'

The last of the carriages pulls up in front of you both and the horses use the pause to chat amongst themselves, for a moment.

'So, it seems everything has turned out for the best, in the end. I'm glad the King presented you with something more substantial than a cheap, crappy medal. I'll have to come visit you sometime, I could do with a vacation. Well, I'd best be off, Winston will be whining for his dinner.' The Old Man opens the door to the carriage and steps in. Before closing the door, he looks at you with almost tearful eyes and says, 'Keep in touch, oh, and remember to aim high, keep your eye on the ball and don't be scared of surprises.'

It is getting dark, now. The carriage rattles away. You watch it go, until it dips out of sight over a grassy hilltop and then you decide to make the long walk home.

You have seen the sunrise, from outside your abode, countless times. The black, speckled sky fading to blue as the rays of the sun creep over the horizon, the darkness of another night recedes before them. You may have seen it yesterday, or the day before, or the day before that, but somehow, always missed it.

The Dream Cast

You
Cassandra Banks
The Commander
Stacey
The Groceries Delivery Courier
The Creature / Your Neighbour
The Woman who lost her Head
The Old Man
The Barmaids
King Berthold IX
Connor MacDonald
The Hibee Geebie Tribe
Winston the Dog
Sergeant Haynes
The Alien Snail Invaders
The Deputy Head Teacher
The Tennis Umpire
The Ball Girl
The Bleep Machine
The Match Spectators
Sydney
Jessica the Mermaid
Toby the Great White Shark
Lieutenant Carter

The Quaint Farmer
The Horse Tremighan - *Nightmare*
The Other Farmers and their Animals
The Woman in the Kitchen
Melbrik and Subren
The Barkeeper
The King's Guards, Courtiers, Musicians and Subjects
Queen Isabella
The Horse Micalwish Nutear - *Whimsical Nature*
The Knight Sir Prancealot
The Horse Rhad Sa Lanis - *Hard As Nails*
The Knight Sir Curidge
The Horse Sevourn Nostidiposi - *Nervous Disposition*
The Knight Sir Agnost
The Horse Dunsed Strom - *Sudden Storm*
The Knight Sir Shipton
The Horse Runbettul Trewa - *Turbulent Water*
The Knight Sir Jovien
The Horse Yalwas Phypa - *Always Happy*
The Knight Sir Veneric
The Horse Sipsang Dwin - *Passing Wind*
The Knight Sir Trepid
The Horse Freddaul Easte - *Dreadful Tease*
The Knight Sir Hardgrip
The Horse Phaevercity - *Hyperactive*
The Magician Pseudomin
The Horse Zaly Stabard - *Lazy Bastard*
The Fire Sprites
The Meta-morphed Alien Woman

Dream Director
Micalwish Nutear

Camera
Sevourn Nostidiposi

Music
Zaly Stabard

Writer
Marleigh Hillier

The End